"I Think I'm Losing My Mind," Nick Nearly Shouted.

"One minute I have a prim-and-proper professor on my hands. The next minute, you've got me about ready to explode," he continued. "You really are . . . something."

"I am?" Emory's voice came out in a husky croak.

"Yes, you are. Maybe it's you and me together. All that chemistry stuff. Whatever it is . . . it's something pretty hot. And you're such a class act. I just didn't want you to think I was some kind of jerk. I just wanted things to happen slower, at a more dignified pace. What you must be used to, I mean . . ." His voice trailed off.

Searching to find the words she needed to say, Emory walked over to where Nick stood and slipped her arms around his waist. Up on tiptoe, she whispered in his ear, "I don't want what I'm used to, Nick. I want you."

Dear Reader:

I can't let February go by without wishing you a Happy Valentine's Day! After all, this is the day that celebrates love and lovers...and it's very special to those of us at Silhouette Books. What better way to celebrate this most romantic of holidays than with Silhouette Desire?

Our "Valentine's Day Man" is sexy *Man of the Month* Roe Hunter in Laura Leone's sinfully sensuous tale, *The Black Sheep*. Roe is a man you're not likely to ever forget, and he really meets his match in Gingie, one of our most *unique* heroines.

Also in store for you is a delightful romance by Dixie Browning, *Gus and the Nice Lady*. Ms. Browning's love stories are always so romantic, so delightful... you won't want to miss this one!

Rounding out February are books by BJ James (her many fans will be pleased!), Anne Cavaliere, Noelle Berry McCue and Audra Adams. Don't miss any of these wonderful books.

And next month...Diana Palmer brings us a new miniseries, *Most Wanted,* revolving around a detective agency. The first book, *The Case of the Mesmerizing Boss,* is also March's *Man of the Month*. I know, you won't be able to wait for it...but March will be here before you know it.

And until March, happy reading!

Lucia Macro
Senior Editor

ANNE CAVALIERE

PRIVATE LESSONS

SILHOUETTE *Desire*®

Published by Silhouette Books New York

America's Publisher of Contemporary Romance

SILHOUETTE BOOKS
300 East 42nd St., New York, N.Y. 10017

PRIVATE LESSONS

ISBN: 0-373-05693-1

First Silhouette Books printing February 1992

Books by Anne Cavaliere

Silhouette Desire

Perfect Timing #328
Squeeze Play #512
Private Lessons #693

ANNE CAVALIERE

worked as a reporter in Denver and Minneapolis before turning to writing as a full-time career. She's also held various positions in the field of advertising in New York. Her interests include sailing, antiques and eavesdropping. She presently lives in Brooklyn, New York.

in the darkness. The same situation soon always on

sword, she noticed, while the other sat with th

pair itself at a dangerous angle ahead.

One

"**O**ur last slide today is a painting of the abstract impressionist period."

Clicking the remote control for the slide projector, Professor Emory Byrd changed the image on the screen beside her. In the blink of an eye, a thirteenth-century masterpiece was replaced by one painted in the twentieth—splashes of pink, violet, and yellow on a swirling green background.

"Can anyone identify the work and painter?" she asked the class.

Perched behind a lectern at the front of the auditorium, Emory waited until a few brave hands slowly rose in the darkness. The same students who always answered, she noticed, while the others sat with their heads bent over their notebooks, clearly terrified she might resort to a random, sneak attack.

Professor Emory Byrd did have a reputation as being somewhat of a terror; a demanding instructor who put out her best and expected the same from her students. But despite her tough exams and assignments, Emory's classes were continually filled to overflow so she had to assume she was doing something right.

Emory finally called on a young woman in the second row.

"*April Fool* by George Polanski?" the girl answered.

"Very good." Emory gave the student an approving nod. Here was one, at least, who would pass the final. "Did everyone hear that? This is Polanski's *April Fool*. Of course, since you have all *dutifully* studied last night's textbook assignment, you already know it was painted in nineteen sixty-three, and that Polanski is considered one of America's foremost abstract impressionists." Her wry, teasing lecture style made her students smile as they frantically scribbled the information in their notebooks. "I'd like you now to note his use of color and light. The balance of shapes, and textures..."

Emory's voice trailed off when she spotted a hand energetically shoot up in the far, shadowy reaches of the lecture hall.

"Yes?" she called out, acknowledging the question. She had noticed him earlier, slipping into one of the back row seats about halfway through the class. Unregistered "crashers" did sit in on her lectures from time to time. Emory didn't mind; she considered it a compliment.

"Excuse me for interrupting you like this, Professor, but..."

"Yes?" she said again, happy to encourage any inquisitive participation.

"I don't get it," he said simply.

The slumping, dozy group was suddenly alert, turning in their seats to get a good look at the upstart. Emory ignored some nervous giggles.

"Get what?" she pointedly inquired. She picked up a pair of large, tortoiseshell glasses and pushed them high on the bridge of her fine, straight nose. She wanted a better look at this guy. Was this some sort of fraternity gag?

"Well, no offense, Professor—" His deep, smooth voice could be heard easily throughout the hall. "—but, let's get real for a minute, okay? It looks to me like this guy Polanski just got a few buckets of paint and threw it on the wall."

The nervous giggles now burst into full-fledged hoots of shock and amusement. Even some voices of agreement, Emory noticed, as if this rabble-rouser had voiced the unspoken opinion of a less courageous contingent.

Straightening to her full five foot, nine inch height, Emory tried to ignore the uproar and leaned closer to the microphone on the lectern.

"Polanski's technique was exactly that," she said simply. "He tossed paint from various containers at a canvas attached to the wall. Sometimes he blended the colors with his hands, or even his feet. Does that answer your question?" she added in a firm, slightly impatient tone.

He shrugged, but to Emory's dismay, his inquiring mind was not yet satisfied. He stood up and she realized then that her heckler was not a boy. Definitely a man. Even through the darkness and distance, some

quality of stubborn—even arrogant—self-possession
was revealed in the mere posture of his broad shoul-
dered figure, facing her with one hand on his hip, the
other gesturing when he spoke. She braced herself for
his next comment.

"What I mean is, what's so great about it? I got one
exactly like it hanging on my refrigerator, by my
nephew Sam." The students roared with laughter at
this last statement, but he continued undaunted. "I
guess the kid's got talent. Turns that stuff out like hot-
cakes."

"Your nephew?" Emory echoed. Was this some
kind of practical joke? But who would stoop this low?
Was this guy just plain crazy?

"He's five. Great kid," he replied. "The thing is,"
he added, sounding very serious and sincere, "maybe
I'm missing something here, but I don't see a heck of
a lot of difference between Sam's stuff and this abstract depressionist's—"

"Impressionist," she corrected him through gritted
teeth.

"Whatever you call it," he finished in a respectful
but extremely stubborn tone. He shrugged his muscular shoulders beneath a leather jacket. "That one you
were talking about first, by the Italian guy, Vito something?"

"Botticelli?" Emory corrected him again. She figured he called *that* one art. The Renaissance masterpiece had more scantily clad young maidens to the
square inch than the latest issue of *Playboy*.

"That's the one," he nodded. "Now that, to me, is
the real thing. You know, *real* art."

Emory groaned quietly, then realized the microphone attached to the podium had broadcasted the

sound. It only encouraged her amused students to laugh even louder. Some were staring at her in open-mouthed shock, breathlessly waiting to see how she would answer this time. Part of her knew she should have ended this exchange about five minutes ago, but another part had unfortunately been mesmerized by the man's outrageous pronouncements. Like a deer hypnotized by the headlights of an oncoming tractor-trailer, she mused.

She was aware, of course, no matter what she said now, this incident would be the talk of the campus within minutes after the class ended. The famous Dr. Emory Byrd, the rising scholarly star of Harvard's prestigious art history department, left babbling at the lectern by some prankster! Emory collected herself. She rarely lost her poise, and never before in front of an entire lecture hall. She would try to emerge from this ridiculous episode with some shreds of dignity intact.

"I am relieved that at least *one* of the slides I've shown today meets *your* demanding critical standards," she finally replied, her sarcastic comeback eliciting even more laughter from the rowdy audience. "The fact remains, however, that *both* paintings are most definitely *real* art. Five-year-old Sam's finger paintings—although they do hang on your esteemed refrigerator—cannot, in the same *breath,* be compared to Polanski's works of genius."

Her class responded with enthusiastic hoots, clapping, foot stamping, cries of "Radical, Doc!" and "Go for it, Professor Byrd!"

She was going for it. Where in the world did this man come off telling *her* what was and was not art?

"Hey, my nephew works hard on those paintings—" he began, attempting a rebuttal. But Emory effectively cut him off. It was her classroom and she would not allow any more of his outrageous remarks to make a mockery of her lecture and the concepts she had been trying to teach these kids all semester.

"These paintings are part of an artistic tradition, a dialogue across the centuries. Each expresses the aesthetic sensibility of the artist's era," she began in a more patient, collected tone. "If Botticelli had never painted *Spring* in the thirteenth-century Italy," she said, clicking the slide projector back to the Renaissance work, "Polanski would not have painted *April Fool* somewhere in Greenwich Village in nineteen sixty-three...."

The bell rang, bringing about an abrupt halt to her explanation. Her students shifted restlessly in their seats, but knew better than to race out of the hall until she had signaled that her lecture was finished.

She sighed and gathered up her notes, feeling frustrated for having wasted so much time on that nincompoop's questions. She shouldn't have humored him. She should have told him point-blank to shut up, or get out. Why did she even dignify his ridiculous comments with a response? But if she didn't even try, her students might have gotten the impression that this wild man had a valid point... which he absolutely did *not!*

"We'll continue with Polanski next class. Please keep up with the reading assignments. And—" she paused, looking up into the shadows to stare directly at the man who had so effectively disrupted her lecture "—I would like to speak with you. Privately."

"Good," he said, coming down the steps two at a time in loose, athletic stride. "I'd like to speak with you privately, too, Professor Byrd."

The lights went up and Emory began gathering her books and notes. A few students lingered to ask questions, taking longer than usual to leave. She suspected they were curious to see what would happen between herself and the mystery art critic.

Her class crasher waited patiently by the lectern, watching her in an assessing way that made her self-conscious, even more uncomfortable than she usually felt under a man's appraising gaze.

Although she was trained to discover and evaluate beauty, Emory remained blind to her own very real and natural loveliness. Compliments hadn't persuaded her. She secretly believed her female friends were only being kind and thought most men would tell a woman anything, if the stakes were high enough.

Emory's older sister Paige had always been the beauty of the family, the daughter destined to shine at debutante balls and eventually marry a suitable young man from a "proper" family. Emory had always been the shy, bookish brainy one. Old family rivalries seemed silly and childish now. Paige had gone through three marriages and Emory had achieved early and astounding academic success. Yet, at age thirty-two, the insecurities and awkward self-image remained. Emory had long ago learned to hide her vulnerability, and even a deeply passionate side to her personality, behind a distant, intellectual air and a sharp sense of humor. As the lights went up, and her outspoken heckler continued to stare, Emory drew those defenses around her like a protective, magic cloak.

Detective Nick Fiore knew he was staring, but he couldn't help it. Professor Byrd at close range was an unexpectedly attractive eyeful. As he watched her answer questions from straggling students she looked up at him briefly, and then away. Angry? Or just not able to figure him out?

He had always had a weakness for blondes and she was an exceptionally classy specimen, her thick honey-colored hair gathered neatly in back and tied with a paisley silk scarf. Loose, he pictured, it would reach an inch or two past her shoulders. He wondered when she wore it like that, to bed perhaps? Her eyes were hazel with golden lights, a distinctive color, noticeable even behind those big, owlish-looking glasses. The flattering blush across her high, finely sculpted cheekbones was her reaction to arguing with him, he guessed, and not makeup. She didn't appear to be wearing a drop of it. Not that she needed any. Her skin was gorgeous. He imagined what more of it might look like, hidden as it was under her rather drab outfit, an oatmeal-colored cashmere sweater, brown tweed wool skirt and brown boots. Totally figure concealing, yet draping her lean, graceful body in a way he found quite intriguing. He imagined this woman had a closetful of outfits like that—expensive, tasteful choices that allowed her to blend into the woodwork whenever she so desired.

He had to watch himself from here on in. He'd already made a mess of things with her, he was sure of it. She was a different sort of woman than he was used to dealing with—a class act all the way. He shouldn't have shot his mouth off. He guessed she was steamed from the look on her face and the way she was slamming her books into a pile. He only hoped she was too well-bred to make a scene.

"Professor Byrd, I owe you an apology—" he began when she finally turned toward him.

"And an explanation," she cut in abruptly. "You did a pretty good job of disrupting my lecture. Were those questions someone's idea of a practical joke?"

"Believe me, my questions were sincere. Even if they sounded sort of...ignorant. I didn't mean to give you a hard time."

Emory could see that her usual position of authority would carry little weight with this man. She sincerely doubted he had any connection to the university. Maybe he was an actor and her practical joke theory was true. With his looks, he could have certainly qualified. She still thought he owed her an explanation, however, even if her initial feelings of outrage were being slowly but surely melted by his smile.

"I don't believe you," she said smoothly. She crossed her arms over her chest. "I'm sure this was a practical joke. Professor Doyle's idea of a good laugh, right?" she asked, naming a not-so-friendly rival in the department.

"Never heard of the guy. Believe it or not, I managed to sound like an uncultured moron without coaching from any of your colleagues," he said with a small laugh. "But thanks for giving me the benefit of the doubt."

Despite her cool response, he continued to smile, a very engaging smile that displayed even white teeth and two deep dimples in his lean cheeks to full advantage. His dark eyes sparkled warmly, his thick lashes an intriguing incongruity in his otherwise utterly masculine face. His dark curly hair, rugged features and muscular build brought to Emory's mind images of Michelangelo's avenging angels and Roman aristocrats. She tried her best, however, to banish such visions.

"I'm not giving you the benefit of anything, at this point," Emory corrected him, managing somehow to hold her ground. "You wasted my time—and more importantly—the class time of my students with your obstreperous questions."

"Look, just calm down a second. Okay?" He ran his hand through his thick curly hair. "I think we've gotten off to a very bad start here—" he said, sounding almost as befuddled as Emory felt.

"Well, here's the finish," Emory offered. "This campus is private property. You are a trespasser as far as I can tell. I think it only fair to warn you I'm about to call security and have you removed. Am I making myself clear?"

"Perfectly," he assented. She was a firebrand once she got started. He had not expected that. Well, it could help later, he reflected. She would need some nerve to get involved in his plan. However, being the object of her ire at this particular moment wasn't exactly a day at the beach.

"Before you run off and put the campus security squad on manhunt alert, you might want to take a look at this—" He dug into the inside breast pocket of his jacket and took out a thick leather wallet. "Detective Nicolas Fiore, Boston Police Department," he said simply, flashing shield and identification. "Which I would have told you sooner, if I could have gotten a word in edgewise."

Emory stared at his identification for a moment. She had begun this conversation partly confused, but now had to admit that she was in a total quagmire.

"You're a policeman?" He nodded. "Now I don't get it," she replied, echoing his own words. She reconsidered that this whole encounter was an elaborate practical joke. But his identification looked real enough. He looked real enough, too. Too good to be true, in fact.

"It's sort of complicated to explain," he said.

"Is this about my parking ticket?" she asked suddenly. "The sign said no parking on Wednesday and Friday and I had parked there on a *Thursday,*" she explained in a rush. "But when I went back to take a photograph of the sign, to contest the ticket, the whole street was torn up for repairs. I've written several letters to the parking violations bureau. It's all documented, I swear it." She finished breathlessly.

"I believe you," Nick assured her. "Don't worry, this has nothing to do with any parking tickets."

"It doesn't?" Emory asked, feeling foolish for having rattled on about her private war with the parking violations bureau.

"No, nothing like that," he said, a hint of a sexy grin causing a strange, tingling feeling in the pit of Emory's stomach. Hunger pains, she told herself.

"Besides you don't exactly strike me as a law-breaking type, Professor," he added, looking at her again in that unsettling way of his, she noted.

"Appearances can be deceiving," she countered.

I certainly hope so, Nick wanted to say. But he decided to hold off on the wisecracks for once and get back to the reason he'd come looking for her in the first place. He'd already made a mess of things by interrupting her class. No need to antagonize the woman any further.

"It's complicated to explain, but basically the police department needs your help in solving a crime," he said quite seriously.

"Solving a crime? Me?" She was incredulous, her mind quickly slipping back to the crazy-person-on-the-loose theory. Maybe he was even carrying a gun. "May I see your identification again?" she asked as calmly as possible.

"Do I really look like some type of con man to you?" he laughed, handing over his ID case again.

"I'm not sure. I've never actually met a real con man," she quietly admitted. Emory took a closer look at his ID. The picture didn't do him justice, she decided. The metal shield looked real enough, but then again, she had only seen these things on TV. She was qualified to assess a work of art worth millions, but police ID badges were completely out of her territory.

He took a small leatherbound notepad out of the back pocket of his jeans and flipped it open. "Mrs. Claire Newland suggested that we contact you," he offered suddenly. He looked at her hopefully, knowing she'd believe him now. "In fact, she more or less volunteered your services."

"Mrs. Newland?" Emory's golden eyes widened. "Are you sure?"

"Look, it's sort of complicated and, also, confidential. Is there someplace private around here where we can talk? Have some coffee, maybe? I'll explain everything to you. I promise," he said, looking too much like that avenging angel, Emory thought, for her to disagree with anything he suggested.

Besides, the lecture hall was starting to fill up again for the next class and Emory thought she had given the student body enough entertainment for one day.

"I can spare a few minutes for coffee," Emory said. She grabbed her loden green wool cape and slipped it around her shoulders, then stuffed her books and notes into a large leather shoulder bag.

"Can I help you with that?" Nick offered. She looked awfully slim to be lugging around that suitcase full of books, he thought. Did she do that every day?

"I can manage, thanks," Emory said quietly. She pushed up the collar of her cape and flipped one end of a gold wool scarf over her shoulder. "I have to be back on campus in about half an hour," she told him as they left the lecture hall.

"This won't take long," he promised, thinking that everything this morning had gone so totally haywire, why did he expect buying this woman a cup of coffee to be any easier?

"There's a coffee shop about a block or so down this way," she suggested as they left the building and crossed Harvard yard.

"Fine, lead the way," he said amiably.

It was a crisp cloudless day in early April. Not quite cold enough for a heavy winter coat, but still chilly when the wind blew down the narrow Cambridge street. The trees were bare, except for a few buds. The sense of spring lurking just around the corner invigorated Emory. Perhaps that was why she had chosen the season as the theme of her lecture today. Unfortunately she had been able to make only a few of her carefully thought-out points—all due to her debate with the man walking beside her. An interruption he still had not explained.

"Just answer one question for me, Detective, and maybe we can forget all about our bad start," Emory asked as she pulled on a pair of brown leather gloves.

"Sure, shoot," he replied. He had zipped his jacket halfway closed and carried a hat in his hand.

"Did you ask me those questions out of honest curiosity today? Or were you just trying to make trouble?"

"I was serious," he assured her. "I never did understand that abstract art racket—"

"It's hardly a racket," she cut in, half laughing and half incredulous at his irreverence.

"Sorry," he apologized again. "See, here I go again. The thing is, I came to your class today thinking I'd just sit in the back and wait for you to finish. Then, before I knew it, I was up on my feet, shooting my mouth off. No harm intended. Just some honest, obstinate ignorance showing," he added. "Does that answer your question?"

"Sure," she said, gathering her cape a bit closer. "But you still think modern art is a racket?" she added, unable to resist one last foray.

"You don't give up, do you?" He laughed and shook his head. "Let's just say that in my admittedly uncultured opinion, any guy who gets a million bucks for throwing paint on the wall has a nice deal going for himself, okay?" Obviously he didn't give up, either, Emory thought. "Is this the place?" he asked as they approached the café. How nimbly he sidestepped the debate when he wished to, she noticed.

"This is it," she said, leading the way inside.

"Great. I could use some coffee." He shot Emory a sidelong glance as he held the door open for her. She unintentionally brushed up against his hard body as she passed through the narrow doorway. It was barely a moment's contact, but she felt herself blushing. She hoped he wouldn't notice.

"I'd never thought tracking down some college professor would make for such a rough morning," he confessed as he shrugged out of his jacket and sat down. "I think I prefer a good, high-speed car chase," he confided with a teasing grin. "No offense, of course."

"No offense taken, I assure you," Emory replied in her best, Swiss finishing-school manner. And she had gone to the best of them.

The coffeehouse was typical of those found near a college campus. Hanging plants hung near the windows and posters decorated the walls. A few students occupied the worn wooden tables, reading books or engaged in avid, caffeine-fueled conversations about the meaning of life and other solemn, philosophical questions. A pretty young waitress came by to take their orders. A mint tea for Emory and an espresso for Nick.

"Okay, Professor. Here's the story," Nick said, quickly getting down to business. "Do you remember when a painting called *Yellow Tulips* was stolen from the Boston Museum of Fine Art last summer?"

"Of course," Emory replied. "It's one of Truffaut's most famous works." The robbery had been widely publicized in newspapers and on TV. Since the painting was valued at several million dollars the theft had made for exciting headlines.

"Well, we think we've got a chance to recover it," he said in a low but excited tone. "The other day, we got a tip that a certain art dealer in New York named Nolan Babcock has the painting and would be willing to make a discreet sale to the right bidder." Emory had heard of Nolan Babcock, but had so far never had any reason to deal with him. Nick's story was giving her goose bumps, however. She was almost afraid to hear how he thought she fit in.

"Go on," she prodded him.

"Since Mrs. Newland is such close friends with the museum director, she has kindly offered to let us use her name when dealing with Babcock. I understand you do some work for her? Sort of a consultant?"

"That's right," Emory said. "I'm the curator for Mrs. Newland's collection. I advise her on her purchases, deal with museums who want to borrow her pieces for exhibitions, speak with dealers. That sort of thing."

Claire Newland's world famous art collection was vast and worth a fortune. The collection included paintings, sculptures and antiquities. Emory was young to have earned such a coveted position, but her knowledge, taste and extreme sensitivity to fine art had won her Mrs. Newland's unquestioning trust and admiration.

"And Mrs. Newland owns a few paintings by this artist, Truffaut, already, right?"

"One painting and a small bronze figure," Emory explained. This still didn't explain how she was to be involved.

"Well, here's where you come in . . . if you want to, I mean." Nick stirred some sugar into his small white cup of thick, black coffee. Emory could feel her heart thudding wildly and hoped he couldn't hear it.

"Our plan is real simple," Nick said. "We figure that you can contact Babcock and hint around about this painting, as if you want to buy it for Mrs. Newland. He's not going to get suspicious because he already has a list of people like Mrs. Newland who would even be in the market for it, right?"

"I suppose," Emory agreed. She didn't know exactly how a crook went about selling a stolen painting, but a list seemed like a logical possibility in the process.

"Well, you negotiate some price, get him to deliver up here in Boston and bingo—we've collared the sucker. Piece of cake," he summed up, sipping his coffee.

"I'm going to deal with Babcock, sort of undercover, is that it?" she asked him after a moment.

"More or less. The police force—yours truly in particular—will be with you every step of the way, of course," he assured her. "We thought that I could pose as your assistant, at least during the first meeting down in New York. Do you think Babcock will buy a situation like that?"

"I suppose," Emory replied. Her voice inflection must have hinted her wariness and her natural inclination to slow down Detective Fiore's persuasive momentum. He was already soliciting her opinion on the scheme's fine points and she hadn't even agreed to take part.

"Hey, don't look so worried. It's not exactly hazardous duty," he assured her. "Not like the cop shows you see on TV."

"I don't watch much television," Emory said.

"No, I don't suppose you do, Professor." Emory would have preferred that he drop her title. But his playful grin told her that he was only teasing. "I can't give any guarantees, of course, but I think Babcock will fold pretty easily."

Emory nodded. Nick simply smiled at her and took another sip of his dark, fragrant coffee. The coffee, she noticed, was about the same rich shade of brown as his eyes. Eyes that now watched her carefully across the small table, trying to gauge her response to his proposition, she guessed. Emory decided she could trust Nick Fiore to protect her. She had no doubt he possessed the quick reflexes and intuitive savvy that could make all the difference in a dangerous situation. Not that this episode would be really dangerous. Certainly more exciting than her quiet, ivory tower life-style, however. That was for sure.

The whole proposition was pretty mind-boggling. You never knew what was going to happen when you got up in the morning, that was for sure. She had expected nothing more exciting today than her new issue of *American Art Scene* in the mailbox when she got home.

"This is your case?" she asked him.

"I'm heading up the operation," he said nodding.

"So recovering stolen artwork is a specialty of yours?" Emory asked, trying to phrase the question as diplomatically as possible.

Nick looked as if he might laugh, but didn't.

"Believe it or not, the precinct doesn't get many opportunities to orchestrate stings on New York art dealers. It's usually something more along the lines of a holdup, drug bust, mugging, stabbing, stolen car, some slime ball turns up stiff in a dumpster...." He rambled on conversationally. "No, I would say that recovering priceless stolen paintings is very low on the list of my specialties."

He was still smiling at her. The man had patience and a quirky sense of humor. Emory would grant him that much. This assignment was sort of a vacation for him, she guessed. He must have thought that she was hopelessly naive and out of touch with the real world. She had to admit, that compared to the world he moved in, she was.

"Just curious," she said. She slipped off her glasses and wiped them with a tissue.

When she looked back up, she caught him watching her and she totally forgot what she had planned to ask next. He had that unreadable look on his face again. What in the world did he think of her? she wondered. And why do you care so much? she had to ask herself. Probably thought she was some sort of sexless bookworm. She could imagine the type of women he was attracted to. The *opposite* type from her, she was sure. He didn't spend much time talking to his girlfriends about abstract impressionism, she'd be willing to bet on that.

Turning her wandering thoughts back to Nick's plan, she finally remembered her question.

"How do you know Babcock won't try to sell a forgery?"

"We don't." He shrugged. "But Mrs. Newland said you'd know if the painting was real or not."

"I suppose I could determine if the work in question was a genuine Truffaut, Detective."

"Call me, Nick," he said, grinning at her. Then he leaned over and whispered, "Generally speaking, it's a whole lot healthier if everybody in the room doesn't know I'm a cop."

"Oh, of course," she said, feeling rather guileless for not realizing that point. "My first name is Emory, by the way."

"Yes, I know. Interesting."

"It's my maternal grandmother's maiden name. She was a suffragette."

"I wouldn't doubt it," he replied, his dark eyes dancing with a teasing light. But before she could summon up an appropriate comeback, he said, "We'll need to go down to New York together to meet Babcock. Any objection to that?''

He was watching her expression. Did he wonder how she felt about working so closely with him? He hardly struck her as a man who felt the least bit unsure of himself with women.

"No, that won't be any problem," she said finally.

"Good. It's all settled, then," he said brightly.

"Not quite. I didn't exactly agree to anything yet," Emory reminded him.

"Look at it this way," he prodded her. "You can do your civic duty, help recover a stolen masterpiece and get a free weekend in New York with one of Boston's finest. The department doesn't offer these special deals to just anybody," he added.

Emory fiddled with her mug of cold tea, trying to gather her thoughts. The way his black sweater molded "one of Boston's finest's" muscular chest and shoulders was so distracting to her at that moment, she could not think clearly. She had a very sensitive eye for form, Emory reminded herself. It has nothing to do with him personally. Yet she had to admit that it was not merely his looks that affected her, but his powerful, distinctly masculine personality. He was different from the men she knew and she found the notion of spending so much time with him both exciting and a little scary.

Emory didn't know what to say. It had all come at her so fast. She had never been one to make snap decisions about important matters.

"I have to think it over," she answered honestly. She looked down at her watch and checked the time. "I'd better be getting back," she added. "I have a class to teach in a few minutes."

She stood up and put on her cape. Nick tossed a few bills on the table and picked up his jacket.

"Anything I'd be interested in?" he asked with a perfectly innocent look on his face.

"Are you trying to blackmail me?" she asked, slipping on her glasses again.

"I do whatever it takes to get the job done, Emory," he said, saying her name in a disturbingly familiar way.

And if it took flirting with a schoolmarmish art history professor, he'd do that, too, she reflected. She walked out of the café a few steps ahead of him, feeling foolish for being even the slightest bit attracted to him.

Out on the sidewalk, a sharp breeze whipped a few strands of hair across her eyes. Emory hugged her shoulder bag closer and stared up at Nick. In his wide-brimmed fedora and leather jacket he looked like a dark, handsome version of Indiana Jones. But what role did that cast her in if she agreed to embark on this adventure with him?

"I want to give you my card," he said, digging through his pockets again for his ID case. He took out a card and wrote on the back of it. "Here's my home number, too. Call me anytime. I need to know by tomorrow if you're in on this."

"Okay," she nodded, staring down at his card.

"And even if you decide not to help us, we'd appreciate it if you'd keep this conversation in strictest confidence."

"Of course," Emory agreed. "Thanks for the tea."

"Thanks for your time." He should have turned and walked away, but for some strange reason he just stood there, his hands jammed into his jacket pockets, his eyes fixed on hers. "I just want you to know that I'll be on my best behavior working with you," he promised in an almost humble tone. As humble as this man ever gets, Emory decided. "I mean, I'll keep my opinions about art to myself."

"Don't worry about it. I find your opinions very...stimulating," Emory assured him, striving to sound tactful, as she had been raised to do in such a situation.

"Stimulating, huh? Well, I guess I've been called worse by a woman after a first date," he replied. "I'll be waiting for your call, Professor." Then he tipped his hat and winked at her, sending a wave of heat through Emory's slim body from head to toe.

Or did she just imagine the wink? she wondered as she watched him quickly disappear into the street's lunchtime crowd. She turned and walked toward the campus, feeling strangely light-headed from the entire encounter. With her hand in the pocket of her cape, she felt the sharp edge of Nick Fiore's card, and Emory knew that she wasn't going to wait until tomorrow to give him her answer. She would call him tonight.

Perhaps she was making a mistake by getting involved in his scheme. It had all sounded so vague, relying on a somewhat fly-by-the-seat-of-your-pants methodology, it seemed to her. But she was not about to pass up this strange, unexpected chance for adventure. Even though the invitation had been delivered by a messenger so unsettling to her peace of mind.

Two

That night Emory called Nick from her office in the art history department. She was sure that she wanted to help the police recover the stolen masterpiece, yet she had to take a deep breath and will herself to punch Nick's number into the phone. She wondered what she was afraid of—the adventure itself? Or the man who had elicited her help?

"Fiore," was his abrupt, businesslike greeting.

"This is Emory Byrd. I'm just getting back to you about the conversation we had this morning."

"Professor Byrd—well, well. I was just talking about you to the captain." His tone had changed abruptly from tough-cop-at-work to hot fudge. Emory half wished he'd return to the clipped voice he'd used to say hello. "You're calling to say that you'll help us, I hope?"

"Yes, I'll do it," Emory replied. Even as she nodded her head, she wondered what she was getting herself into.

"Excellent," Nick replied. "We want to move on this quickly, before Babcock approaches another buyer. The first thing we'd like you to do is set up a meeting with him down in New York for sometime next week. Friday would be best, I think."

"Babcock is exhibiting some paintings by a South American artist, Frieda Salazar. I might call him on the pretext of an interest in her work," Emory suggested.

"Perfect. You're a natural, Professor. I can feel it in my bones. When you've set up the appointment, give me a call and we'll figure out traveling arrangements and so on.... Oh, and don't forget to tell Babcock about your sharp, new assistant...yours truly."

As if she could possibly forget. "I'll tell him your specialty is South American surrealists and their influence on contemporary post-moderns. How's that for a cover story?"

"Sounds great. Let's just hope our conversation doesn't go any further than the number of colors in a deluxe Crayola crayon set."

"I don't even know the answer to that myself." Emory laughed. "How many are in a *deluxe* set?"

"Sixty-four, of course," he replied, sounding amazed at her ignorance on the topic. "For heaven's sake, what are you people teaching there at Harvard?"

"A serious gap in my knowledge, I must admit," Emory replied with mock solemnity. "I am so glad someone was able to finally set me right on the Crayola question. It's a burning issue here in the art history department."

"No problem. And if you have any questions about paint-by-number sets, don't hold back."

"Maybe you could give a guest lecture sometime," Emory said quietly. "I have to go now. I'll let you know when I've set up the appointment with Babcock."

After the call, Emory packed her shoulder bag and headed home. She wondered what she'd gotten herself into. Too much, she reflected early the next morning as she groggily answered the phone.

"Emory? Nick Fiore. Did I wake you?"

Emory glanced at the clock. It was seven-thirty. "Sort of," she croaked.

"Out late on a school night were you?" Nick asked, sounding surprised.

"Late enough," Emory replied testily, wondering how it was any of his business. He probably pictured her grading papers and watching nature shows on the educational channel.

"I just wanted to catch you before you left the house. An important consideration came to mind regarding our plan," Nick said smoothly.

"Yes?" Emory tried to sit upright in bed, but her big orange cat, Leo—short for Leonardo da Vinci—was curled into a cozy ball of fur at her feet. Each time Emory stirred, Leo snuggled in deeper, making it impossible for her to move under the comforter.

"Leo, move over, for goodness' sake," Emory groaned. "You're pushing me off the bed."

Nick coughed politely, reminding her of his presence before she said anything more incriminating. "I hope I'm not...interrupting anything?" he asked diplomatically.

"Uh, no. It's all right, really," she said, purposely not offering an explanation. "What's on your mind?"

"I know I made a joke of it yesterday, but it seems to me that if we're going to tell Babcock I'm your assistant, I'd better be able to talk about more than crayon sets."

"Good point," Emory agreed. She wondered what this was all leading up to. "Is this a warning that you might sit in on my class again today?"

"I wouldn't dare. I need your help too much to risk another scene like yesterday." He laughed.

Emory laughed, too; mainly from sheer relief.

"Would you like to borrow a few books? I've some excellent survey volumes I can loan you."

"That's very nice of you to offer. But I don't have much time lately for reading." He paused and Emory wondered what was coming next. "I was wondering if maybe you could just fill me in? You know, a sort of one-on-one crash course? Nothing too intense, of course. Just the high points."

"Just the high points of twenty centuries of art history?" Emory echoed. "I suppose I could try," she said, running her hand through her bedraggled hair.

"Great," he answered brightly. "I thought we could visit a museum—I'll leave the choice up to you. I'm working tomorrow. How about Sunday afternoon?"

"Sunday?" Emory swung her feet over the edge of the bed. This was sounding more like a date every second. What was going on here?

"I know it's short notice, but if we plan to meet with Babcock next week, we don't have much time to turn me into an art connoisseur. . . . But perhaps you have other plans for the weekend?" he asked pointedly.

"No, it's okay. Sunday will be fine." Emory, out of bed now, twirled in a circle, looking for her bathrobe and inadvertently tangling the phone cord around her ankle. The man got her so flustered it was positively astounding. "Might as well get this over with, I suppose."

"Well, don't get *too* excited, Professor," Nick laughed. "I might get the wrong idea."

Emory didn't know quite how to answer that remark. She was honest enough with herself, however, to admit that she was indeed inordinately excited. He needn't know that, of course, she reminded herself.

They arranged a time for Nick to pick her up and Emory gave him the address.

"I'll be a good student," Nick promised. "You'll be surprised."

"I will be," Emory countered. She had finally located her bathrobe on the antique rocking chair, but the displaced Leonardo had staked it out as his new territory. He was not giving it up without a fight. "Leo—" she murmured, tugging at the robe "—come on. Let go of my robe...."

"Excuse me?" Nick asked abruptly. She pictured him on the other end of the phone line, straining to discern her mumbled cat commands.

"Uh, nothing. See you Sunday," she said quickly, ending the conversation. Now he could really let his imagination run wild until Sunday, she thought as she hung up the phone.

Sunday afternoon Emory's doorbell rang promptly at one. She buzzed Nick in and then waited by the opened front door so that he would have no trouble finding her apartment.

"This is some great old building," he said, glancing around the apartment appreciatively. "Great apartment, too," he added, surveying the high ceilings, gleaming hardwood floors, exposed woodwork and long, elegant windows that allowed midday sunlight and a view of the Charles River.

"The building was once a private home, a mansion owned by one family," Emory explained. "It was broken up into apartments some time ago."

"Can you imagine, one family having a place like this all to themselves?" Nick shook his head. "That's what I call real money," he added.

"Uh, yes," Emory agreed. She neglected to add that her own family still lived in a home a lot like this apartment building on Boston's Back Bay.

Although Emory's taste in art was eclectic, her apartment was primarily decorated with antiques. Most had been in her family for generations—Persian rugs, cloisonné china and Tiffany glass lamps, oil paintings and incidental knickknacks from around the world. Emory felt a bit self-conscious as Nick entered her living room slowly and cautiously, appraising the surroundings. A true detective, she thought.

Finally he stood in the middle of her living room, in front of the carved marble fireplace. "I've never seen so many antiques before," he admitted, stepping closer to the mantel to look at something that had caught his interest. "Maybe in a shop, but not in anyone's house."

"Most of the furniture and paintings were given to me, by my parents and other people in my family," Emory said.

"Inherited, you mean," Nick replied.

"Passed down to my sister and me," Emory amended. She hated the word "inherited"—it made her feel like a character out of a Dickens novel.

"My folks wanted to give me some furniture when they moved to Florida, but the only thing I took was this old rolltop desk of my father's," Nick told her. "He kept it in the back of his store and I always wanted to do my homework there when I was a kid, but he would always chase me away. 'You go home and do your homework in your room, where it's quiet and you can concentrate.'" Nick put on a stern expression as he imitated his father. "But I liked hanging around him. Helping him, waiting on customers. And now I can sit at that desk anytime I want. I always feel like I'm getting away with something. I guess part of me misses hearing him scold me."

Emory laughed. Nick was so natural and open. She found it amazingly refreshing.

"What type of store was it?" she asked. She pictured him suddenly as an energetic, dark-haired little boy, not quite a troublemaker, but no angel, either.

"Hardware, right in our neighborhood, the north side," he said, mentioning Boston's Little Italy.

"That must have been an interesting place to grow up in."

"Oh, indeed it was," he assured her. "How about you? Were you raised in Boston?"

"Yes, I was. Well, until my parents sent my sister and me away to boarding school."

"Boarding school." Nick shook his head. "That sounds a little scary. If you're a little kid, I mean."

"Well . . . it was," Emory admitted.

He was so easy to talk to, for some reason she found herself confessing all sorts of things that she'd never meant to say. She was normally such a private person that it surprised her. She realized that the interest he seemed to show in her probably caused her to tell more than she meant to. But it wasn't anything personal on his part, she told herself. It had something to do with his job. He probably had a special way of getting people to talk. After all, he was an investigator.

"This is a very interesting piece," he said then, changing the subject. A small, Oriental figurine on the mantel had captured his attention. Carved in ivory, it was the figure of a naked woman reclining on a couch of carved rosewood.

"It's Chinese, several centuries old, although not strictly decorative," Emory explained. She moved the sculpture on the mantel so that Nick could see it better. "These figures served a practical purpose when they were made. At one time doctors and practitioners of acupuncture used them to treat women patients. A woman would use the figure to point out where it hurt on her body, thereby protecting her modesty."

"It's very lovely," Nick said sincerely.

"Would you care to hold it?" she offered, picking the figure up off the miniature rosewood couch.

"Oh, no. I'd be afraid to drop it."

"Don't be silly," Emory said. She picked up his hand, which he spread out flat. With her hand hovering lightly beneath his, she placed the figure across his open palm.

"It's so light and delicate," he said. "I thought it would feel heavier."

"Ivory is far lighter than it looks," Emory said. "This happens to be an unusual example because of the figure's position and expression on her face," she pointed out. It was an unusually sensual pose and expression, which was what Emory had wanted to say, but somehow the explanation caught in her throat.

"Yes, she looks very... relaxed," Nick replied. The tip of his index finger skimmed lightly from the figure's smooth, elongated neck, across her shoulder and down one white leg. Emory heard herself draw in a quick breath. He looked up from the figure directly into Emory's eyes, then down at her half parted lips. She was sharply aware of their nearness and the feeling of his rough, warm hand in her own. For the briefest second she imagined he was about to lean over and kiss her. She blinked the image away.

"Sorry," he said finally. "That was dumb of me. I guess I never learned 'look but don't touch.'"

"That's all right. It's not that delicate," Emory replied lightly. She knew very well that her reaction to watching Nick stroke the sculpture had little—or nothing—to do with being afraid it might break. She wondered if the same rule would apply to her—would he soon forget 'look but don't touch'?

Then she was surprised at the direction of her wandering thoughts. Surprised that this man—who clearly had about as much in common with her as a visitor from another planet—affected her so powerfully. And he hadn't even touched her. She'd never quite experienced such a situation before.

Nick quickly and gently placed the figure back on its stand and then looked back at Emory with a slight smile.

"Well, I guess you've just gotten your first lecture of the day," Emory said, trying to put their meeting back on a more "official" ground. "Let me know if I'm rambling on too much."

"To the contrary, Professor. This is shaping up to be a very enlightening afternoon."

"I hope so." Emory glanced up at him with a nervous smile, then headed for the door. She was also learning something today, about herself and men.

Three

___

Nick's car, a shiny black, two-seater Jeep, was parked right in front of her building. Emory had to step up to get inside, but once she was seated it was quite comfortable. The Jeep had a sturdy "no frills" feeling that suited Nick perfectly, she decided. Even the cargo area in back, which looked like the inside of a gym locker. Emory spotted a pumped-up basketball, a mostly deflated soccer ball, a hockey stick and a bicycle helmet, which she imagined must come in handy for any number of other uses considering Nick's athletic pursuits.

No wonder he was in such good shape. When he wasn't out chasing criminals, he was training for a triathlon. She was not the athletic type. All in the name of being "a good sport", she'd swung her fair share of tennis rackets, or tumbled down snowy hillsides on skis all through high school and college. But Emory had long ago given up such pursuits, which she considered rather pointless. Her idea of exercise now was a brisk walk downtown to her favorite bookstore-café.

"Where to?" he asked as he started up the engine.

"I thought we'd go to the Gardner Palace first, then right across the street to the Museum of Contemporary Art. This way you'll get a good sampling of different eras. Then if we have any extra time, we can drop into a few galleries on Newberry Street."

"Newberry Street, too?" Underneath his forced smile she could discern him secretly wincing.

"I'm just trying to cover the high points. If we wanted to do this right, we would start with Mesopotamian cave paintings."

"Mesopa—? You want to run that one by me again?"

"Mesopotamian cave paintings," Emory repeated slowly.

"Like caveman graffiti, right?" He glanced over at her as he steered around a corner.

"In a way," she replied hesitantly. She didn't care much for the comparison, but didn't want to squelch his interest so early in the day. "Of course, such early examples are very rare."

"Of course," Nick nodded. "I bet those Mesopotamian guys had a hell of a time getting hold of the spray paint."

"You're not taking this very seriously, are you?" Emory shot him a sidelong glance. He was surprisingly serious in her apartment, discussing the ivory sculpture. But out here, he was more of what she had expected. Why did she even suggest this outing if all he was going to do was hand her wisecracks all day?

"Sorry—" He shook his head, a mischievous smile edging up the corners of his mouth. "I promised to be a good student, didn't I?"

"As a matter of fact, you did," Emory reminded him.

"And you didn't have to come out here today with me and do this," Nick pointed out. "You could have handed me a stack of books and sent me on my way."

"That would have been one solution," Emory agreed, looking straight ahead.

"For all I know, you could have canceled plans. You could have been spending the day with friends.... Your friend *Leo,* for instance?" he added meaningfully.

"My friend Leo?" Emory didn't understand what he meant for a moment. Then it came to her. "Maybe—" she said slyly, trying to hide a laugh. "We do spend a lot of time together on the weekends."

Nick did not look at all pleased at her answer. He stared into the traffic, his brows knitted into a frown.

"Does he mind that you're helping the police with this case?" Nick asked.

"Well—" Emory hesitated, wondering how long she should keep up this silly pretext about some phantom paramour. A bit longer, she decided. She liked having the upper hand with Nick Fiore for a change and felt their little "misunderstanding" over Leonardo's companionship would serve as protection of sorts for her in the event that... Well, future transgressions of the look-but-don't-touch rule were not entirely out of the question, were they?

"Leo and I have a very...special relationship," she said finally. "He really doesn't have much say about my activities," Emory said lightly.

"So he won't mind you going down to New York for the weekend with me, then? That's all right with him?" Nick prodded.

"Leo doesn't ask any questions. I really am free to do as I please. He's very easygoing that way. He'll manage just fine for himself while I'm away," Emory replied, a glint of mischief in her eye as she silently added, as long as Leo has a full bowl of cat crunchies and a clean litter box.

"Sounds like a nice relationship. A modern arrangement," Nick replied gruffly, his tone belying that he thought it was good at all. "Although, I must say that maybe I'm not the most liberated guy in the world; but...uh, forget it. None of my business," he fairly muttered to himself as he deftly maneuvered the Jeep through a clump of traffic.

Reading his meaningful look, Emory guessed that he was about to say he'd be asking more than a few questions. She could bet on that. For a brief moment she tried to imagine what it might be like, being held accountable that way by Nick Fiore. What sort of demands did he make upon his woman and what exactly did he offer in return? She imagined him passionate, possessive, yet protective and utterly true. She guessed he demanded everything, yet gave all of himself in return. After a moment she didn't want to think of it at all.

"You had better make the next right," Emory suggested calmly. "We just missed the turn for the museum."

Emory thought Nick knew where they were going, but perhaps he had been distracted by the conversation. He suddenly yanked the wheel and made an impressive, hairpin U-turn across two lanes of oncoming traffic. Emory unintentionally tilted toward him, their shoulders cozily rubbing as she reflexively squeezed her eyes closed. The Jeep swerved through the about-face maneuver and then swerved around the corner. She could not recall having as exciting a ride in a moving vehicle since she took her niece and nephew to a theme park last summer.

"Here we are," Nick announced cheerfully as the museum came into sight. "Safe and sound," he said, swooping into an empty parking space.

If he ever decided to quit the police force he could always get a job as a stunt driver, Emory thought. However, she thought it best not to voice the observation aloud.

As they entered the Gardner Palace, Emory explained to Nick how the phenomenally wealthy Mrs. Gardner had an entire Florentine palace transported, piece by piece, to America and reassembled in Boston. Surrounded by her vast art collection, she had lived for many years in a private apartment in the three-story stone palace. At her death, it was her wish that the palace be opened to the public with the proviso that the museum ensure every single object—paintings, furniture, sculpture, objets d'art—remained *exactly* as she had left them.

Emory led Nick through the various rooms and told him about the many masterpieces displayed there. Nick treated Emory to his uncensored, but often insightful impressions. Rembrandt? Too much brown. Goya? Too big for the average living room, that was for sure. Sargent's portrait of Mrs. Gardner? To Nick, the great lady looked like "a real piece of work." She shuddered to imagine any of her colleagues overhearing this

afternoon's "lesson" with her new student. She was
secretly relieved to reach the last room in the palace and
wondered if she should even bother with the next stop
on her list.

Nick and Emory ended their tour on the second floor
stone balcony. For a moment they stood silently, side
by side, looked down at the garden and milling crowd
below.

"The paintings didn't do that much for me," Nick
admitted, "but I do really like this place. It makes me
feel far away," he said thoughtfully. "Far away from
Boston, that's for sure."

"Me, too," Emory agreed. At that moment she was
surprised to be so in sync with the feeling Nick had
voiced. "I feel as if I'm in Italy. Or Spain, perhaps."

"You sound as if you get around, Professor."

Emory shrugged. "I've done my share of traveling,
I guess," she said lightly. "I studied at the Sorbonne in
Paris for a year before I came to Boston to finish my
dissertation."

"For your Ph.D., you mean?" he asked, as if he
were talking about some strange custom of an exotic
tribe.

Emory just nodded and looked down at the garden
again. Every time she and Nick shared even a brief
moment of closeness, something cropped up in the
conversation to show her just how different in background and interests they really were. It was one thing
to find a man attractive—even compellingly attractive—as she was beginning to feel about Nick. But
there was a lot more to it all than chemistry. Emory had
learned that the hard way.

Across the street, at Boston's Museum of Contemporary Art, Emory had her work cut out for her. She

explained how the Impressionists had theories about light and color, the Cubists had theories about space and dimension.

Nick seemed to like Van Gogh and some of the French Impressionists like Monet. He nodded politely in front of a Picasso, created in his Cubist phase, then turned to her with his eyes crossed. Surprisingly enough, one of his favorites seemed to be a Campbell's soup can portrait by Andy Warhol. He stood in front of the silk screen, his hand thoughtfully rubbing his chin.

"You look like you're thinking serious thoughts," Emory observed.

"I am," Nick assured her. "I'm thinking about how this very modern work reminds me of some great Italian masterpieces."

"You are?" Emory replied, unable to hide the incredulous note in her voice. Could it be that the past three hours of her informative droning about art history had actually penetrated Nick's sharp but somewhat resistant brain? What a victory for her side, she secretly reveled.

"What sort of comparison would you make between this Warhol and the Italian masters?" she asked him eagerly.

"Tomato. See?" He pointed to the flavor of the soup in the Warhol painting. "It's really making me hungry. Ready for a bite to eat?"

Emory was surprised. Partly by his answer and also because she didn't know dinner was also on the agenda.

"Only if you have the time," she said, glancing at her watch. Didn't he have a date or something? she wondered. After all, they had spent the entire day together.

"Maybe you have to get home for some reason?"

"Uh, no. I don't," she said simply.

"Great, I know the perfect place to conclude this art tour, Professor," Nick said very seriously. "Over in the north end."

"The north end?" Emory didn't quite understand. The north end had some historic monuments, but Emory wasn't aware of any art museums or galleries there.

"That's right. I'm going to show you some real Italian masterpieces. A plate of shrimp Marinara, on a bed of fresh linguine that could make Michelangelo's mouth water," he said very seriously.

"Sounds like an interesting composition," she replied, playing along with his joke.

After another hair-raising, but blessedly brief ride in Nick's Jeep, Emory found herself on the streets of the north end. The old buildings and narrow winding streets made it one of the city's most interesting neighborhoods. The streets were filled with eateries ranging in elegance from pizza parlors to those with canopied entrances and limousines parked at the door. Nick seemed to know exactly where he wanted to go and did not even bother to consult her.

"Here we are—Café Fiorenza," he announced as he parked the Jeep.

"Looks like a long wait," Emory said, noticing the long line that stretched out the doorway into the street.

"Don't worry, we'll get a table in a minute," Nick assured her. "Best calamari in town," he promised her.

"I don't think I ever tasted ... calamari," Emory replied honestly as he ushered her through the crowd at the door. His broad hand resting lightly at the small of her back was distracting and prevented Emory from worrying that her escort was about to force her into a culinary misadventure.

"Isn't that some sort of fish?" she asked Nick as he hustled her through the line of waiting diners.

"Baby squid. Very tender and sweet," he assured her. "Much tastier than Conchiglie."

"Oh," Emory said simply. She feared to ask what Conchiglie was. Some squiggly, tentacled relative, she had no doubt.

At the head of the line, a silver-haired man in a dark suit greeted Nick with a broad smile and handshake. Before Emory knew what was happening, she and Nick were led to a table in the quieter, rear section of the restaurant, where long, old-fashioned windows framed a view of a courtyard.

"You got to come back to my place when you want a good meal, right?" Nick's friend said as he handed them both menus.

"Unless I cook it myself, Louie," Nick replied with a laugh.

"I'm waiting for you to quit the police, so you can come work in my kitchen," Louie replied.

A single look from Louie and busboys scurried over with water and bread. Emory felt like visiting royalty.

"No way, pal. It's too dangerous back there," Nick said amiably. "A guy could get seriously hurt."

"Wise guy, huh?" Louie gave Nick a friendly pat on the back. "You ever eat Nick's cooking, Emily?" Louie asked Emory.

"Her name is Emory," Nick corrected his friend.

"I—uh... I've never had the pleasure," she replied, glancing quickly over at Nick.

"Yeah—well, a lady better be careful when this guy gets in the kitchen," Louie warned her. "I heard about a woman who took one bite—" Louie pantomimed the gesture "—and she proposed marriage to him."

"Louie!" Nick burst out laughing. "Beat it, will you? Don't pay any attention to him," he said to Emory.

"Hey, I'm not kidding," Louie insisted. "I know it's hard to believe when you take a look at his ugly mug." Louie shrugged. "But some women like him."

"Don't mind him," Nick said after Louie had finally left them alone. "We've known each other a long time. He just likes to tease me in front of the friends I bring in here."

In front of his dates, Emory knew he really meant to say. There were probably a lot of them and she wouldn't doubt that Nick had even received a proposal of marriage . . . or two. Although, probably not as Louie had described it.

"So, you're a gourmet cook, too?" Emory said.

"You mean in addition to my other accomplishments? Like . . . art connoisseur?"

"And ace driver," Emory felt obliged to add.

Nick laughed. "I do like to fool around in the kitchen. Mostly recipes my mother taught me." He took an olive off the platter in the middle of the table and popped it into his mouth.

"It's an unusual combination," Emory admitted. "Police work and cooking."

"I'm pretty intense about it, but it's really relaxing for me, too. I think because my life is on the line in my work, I really relish those everyday, simple pleasures other people might take for granted—a fine bottle of wine, a good meal, interesting conversation with an attractive woman..." His voice trailed off and Emory found herself staring into his dark gaze.

Did he add making love to that list of simple pleasures? Emory was certain he must and she was equally certain at that moment that Nick was an intense and passionate lover.

"I suppose I've heard that said," Emory replied, her voice coming out in a husky tone. "I mean, that people who have dangerous jobs experience life more intensely. It makes sense."

"Maybe." Nick nodded. "I don't know if it has so much to do with a job, though. Seems to me some people just don't know the first thing about how to enjoy themselves," Nick said, glancing up at her over his menu.

Did he put her in that category? she wondered. Someone who didn't know how to enjoy life? The possibility was vaguely insulting, but she had to admit that there would be some truth to the charge. Emory had often felt that she spent too much time working, and that her pursuit of excellence in her career was in fact an avoidance of life, a place for her to hide and avoid trying new challenges. The perfect refuge from octopus salad and men like Nick Fiore.

A waiter had brought a bottle of red wine to the table and Nick filled their glasses. Emory took a hearty gulp for courage.

"I think sometimes people are just scared."

"Scared? Scared to enjoy themselves?" Nick answered in an interested but puzzled tone.

"They don't realize it, of course. Maybe they think they're dedicated to their work...and maybe they are. But..." She was starting to feel self-conscious. The explanation was beginning to sound like a self-description and she suddenly wasn't at all sure she wanted to expose so much of herself to Nick. "Well, I suppose it depends on how a person was raised ... and that sort of thing. That's what a psychologist would say, I guess."

"I guess," Nick agreed. She looked up at him briefly, then down at her menu. He was watching her expression in the flickering candlelight and she was uncomfortable under his scrutiny.

"Well, here's to simple pleasures," he said, touching his glass to hers. "That's my philosophy."

Emory smiled and tasted her wine again. He was proving to be a bit of an enigma, she thought. When they'd first met, she thought she had him all figured out. But right now, she wasn't so sure.

"See anything you like on the menu?" he asked her.

"Hmm—" Emory hesitated, then with the corner of her mouth lifting in a grin, she said, "I think I'll try the calamari since you recommend it so heartily."

"Good choice." Nick laughed, looking pleased to see her take up his small challenge. "Besides, if it's too spicy for you, you can always pass it my way," he suggested amiably.

"That's right, you're a tough guy. You can take the heat, right?"

"That's right." Nick smiled agreeably. "Especially from a dish of Louie's pasta. Hey, Joe—" Nick called out to a harried-looking waiter. "How about taking our order already? We're starving to death over here."

A few of the other customers turned around to look at Nick, and Emory felt her cheeks getting red and warm. Their waiter, however, did not take offense in the least, greeting Nick with a friendly handshake as he took down their order.

When the food arrived, Emory eyed her dish with apprehension. She suddenly regretted wanting to give Nick the impression that she was so adventurous. Nick must have read her mind, for as she stared down into her mysterious-looking food, he said, "What do you think?"

"I think something down there is waving at me," she barely whispered. He started laughing. "I mean it. Right there, under that chunk of tomato."

Emory pointed down at her plate to a piece of food that appeared to be a miniature octopus tentacle.

"Now, now—Professor," Nick chided her. "I thought you said you were up to this? Was that just loose talk?"

"I did say that, didn't I?" Emory looked him squarely in the eye, then with a deep breath, she carefully avoided any tentacles and took a minuscule forkful to her mouth. She had once read that if you held your breath, you couldn't taste. It was hard not to breathe while she chewed and swallowed. Especially with Nick watching her so intently. Finally she gulped it down and actually allowed herself to taste it.

With Nick's gaze still fixed on her, her look of apprehension was quickly replaced by one of surprised pleasure.

"So? What do you think?"

"This is...good," Emory admitted, taking another taste. The red sauce was hot and spicy, filled with onions, garlic and delicious-tasting herbs. Once she got past the way it looked, the squid was quite mild and sweet tasting. "Really good," she repeated, going back for another bite with gusto.

"Glad you like it. Louie would have been crushed if we sent it back to the kitchen," he added in a confidential tone, "and my waistline would be better off without two dinners. Gets tough to keep in shape when you're an old guy pushing forty," he admitted with a sigh.

As far as Emory could see, the "old guy" sitting across from her was definitely meeting the challenge.

She dug her fork into her pasta once more, clumsily scooping up another mouthful. When she looked, Nick was watching her again, a gleeful, teasing look in his eyes.

"Is something the matter?" She quickly patted her mouth with her napkin, thinking she must have sauce all over her face.

"With all due respect," Nick began gently, "I am sure you know about a million times more than I do about art and history and God only knows what. But I believe one area of your education has been sadly neglected."

"It has?" Emory sat up straight. She couldn't imagine what he might be referring to.

Nick nodded sagely. "Didn't anyone ever teach you how to eat spaghetti?"

"What do you mean? I know how to eat spaghetti," she said with a light laugh.

"No you don't." He shook his head emphatically. "Believe me. I've seen this before. You try to fake it, fiddling around the plate with your fork, hoping the spaghetti will stay on and won't fall off before you get it to your mouth," he said, simultaneously doing an exaggerated, but nonetheless fair, imitation of Emory trying to tackle her pasta.

"I admit it." Emory shook her head with mock remorse. "You've caught me red-handed, Detective. Is

there some kind of summons I get for this?'' she asked
tartly.

"There should be," Nick replied. Clearly, here was
a man who took linguine quite seriously. She'd do well
to remember it, too. With a ceremonious flourish, he
took his fork in one hand and his spoon in the other.
"I'd be happy to share the ancient Roman secret
of properly transporting spaghetti from plate to
mouth...if you're interested."

"Oh—please do," Emory implored him. "I'm fascinated. Honestly." She sat up, giving him her undi-
vided attention.

"Fork in the right hand, spoon in the left." He
demonstrated with his own utensils. "Hold the fork
loose enough to twirl, the spoon, a firm base with a low
center of gravity. That's the basic principle here."

"Oh, I didn't realize there was so much physics involved. Go on." Emory nodded, a slight smile twisting up the corner of her mouth. She had to admit it, an
extensive education and world travel had somehow
missed this information.

"You pick up a few strands." He demonstrated on
his own pasta. "Twirl, pressing into the spoon," he
said, doing just that. "And presto—" He showed her
the results. "It's all neat and tidy, no embarrassingly
loose ends to slurp up." He popped the forkful into his
mouth and smiled.

Emory honestly hoped she had not been slurping up
her loose ends prior to this instructive tip.

"Looks easy enough when you do it," she said. She
took up her fork and spoon exactly as Nick had showed
her and tried it. She had to admit, it was a lot neater.

"Very good." He smiled at her. "You're a quick
study."

"Thanks." She twirled again, and somehow didn't manage it quite as neatly as Nick had. "I can see that there's more to this than meets the eye."

"Don't worry, it takes years to perfect a technique," he said encouragingly.

"I wasn't that worried," Emory said smartly. "But thanks for the lesson."

"My pleasure. It's the least I can do to repay you for my whirlwind art tour today."

"Think you'll remember any of it?" Emory asked him. "I mean, if Babcock asks you questions."

"Don't worry, I'll do fine," Nick reassured her.

"If you say so," she replied, taking a sip of her wine. He looked rather smug, she thought. But she didn't doubt that Babcock would figure out Nick didn't know a Picasso from a pizza. Well, it was his problem wasn't it?

"As you pointed out only moments ago, Professor, I'm a man of many talents. One of the most valuable, fast-talking my way around guys like Babcock."

Or women like me? she added silently. Her glass was empty and Nick reached over to fill it, and then fill his own.

"Is that something they teach when you join the police force? How to fast-talk people?"

Emory didn't know quite why she asked the question in quite that way. It was actually rude, and unlike her. But it just popped out. She'd have to watch the wine, she thought. It was stronger than she realized and she had never been able to drink much without doing or saying something foolish.

Nick didn't seem the least bit insulted. Surprised maybe, but pleased, she thought, by her bluntness.

"Now there's an interesting question, Professor. I see I have a curious student in my class."

Emory normally hated it when people addressed her by her title outside of the classroom. But somehow from Nick, it was amusing and sounded almost affectionate. Although, she corrected herself, they had hardly known each other long enough for it to be that.

"When you train to be a police officer, you learn a lot of useful things. Practical, nuts-and-bolts lessons about making it through a normal business day."

Emory imagined much of his normal business day involved crime scenes, shoot-outs, car chases and situations she'd only seen in the movies.

"When you actually *are* a police officer," Nick continued, "you learn even more useful skills. On-the-job training, you might call it." He smiled, patting his mouth with his napkin, which he folded neatly by his plate. "Now, conning a guy like Babcock... well, I'd say that even if I hadn't chosen my particular avocation, I'd have developed a natural ability, let us say, for that particular and most useful skill. My job, I suppose, has simply brought out these natural talents."

"I see." Emory smiled at his eloquent and amusing explanation. She wondered why he had chosen police work. He was obviously quite intelligent, with personality and charm to spare. He could have been successful at most anything he tried, she thought.

"Why did you join the police force, Nick?" Emory finally asked him.

"Well, that's another good question," he said. He looked into her eyes for a moment before replying, then down at his glass of wine. "Don't you mean, what kind of person wants to be a cop, right? It's sort of in the same league as working in the post office, or being a bus driver, right?''

Although his voice was still smooth and low, Emory felt a sudden and distinct shift in his mood. Her question had clearly struck a sensitive nerve. He retreated from her, closed off some part of himself, like a curtain swiftly drawn. She wondered if something in her tone had suggested that she thought he might have done better than choosing the police force. Emory bit down on her bottom lip. Was she really as much of a snob as Nick thought? God, she hoped not.

''No... I didn't mean it that way. Not at all,'' she replied.

''It's okay.'' He shrugged a broad shoulder and forced a tight smile. ''We can at least be straight with each other, Professor,'' he said, looking up at her again. This time when he used her title, it sounded harsh and disdainful. ''It's best to get this stuff out in the open, right from the start. After all, we're partners on this case. We ought to be honest with each other.''

''Yes, we ought to be,'' she agreed. To be perfectly honest with him, she had to admit that she had only asked the question because of her attraction to him. An attraction she had barely admitted to herself. Their day together had been fun...the most fun she had had with a man in a long time. Emboldened by the many glasses of red wine, Emory gamely plunged ahead.

''I only asked because I was curious about you, your past. Who you are. I'd just like to know more about you...'' Her voice trailed off.

There, she'd done it. All but admitted her heart was doing a somersault every time he smiled at her over the

candlelight at this much too small and intimate table.
Well, he was sure to get a good laugh out of it.

He didn't say anything to her. Barely looked at her.
Finally he shook his head and let out a long audible
sigh.

"I'm sorry," he said finally. The look in his warm
brown eyes melted something down inside her. "I
shouldn't have snapped at you that way. I wasn't
thinking..." He paused and Emory had the distinct
feeling he was thinking too much. Too much about
something or someone in his past that she had reminded him of?

"It's all right," she said.

"No, it's not really. It's a sore spot for me, I guess.
We get a lot of flack about our work. I was on auto-
matic. I hope you'll forgive me for shooting my mouth
off? ...Forgive me *again,* I mean?"

"Sure—" The way he was looking at her, Emory
would have forgiven him for just about anything. She
felt suddenly flustered under his warm attentions.
"Let's just forget it, okay?" Emory offered.

"Not so fast," he said with a gentle smile. He
reached across the table and covered her hand with his
own. "So, you want to know more about me, huh?"

Nick's warm gaze and seductive tone had caused a
sudden wave of electricity to go zinging across Emory's
limbs from head to toe. A lump, the size of a forkful of
linguine, lodged in her throat when she tried to answer
him.

"Well—hmm...yes," Emory fairly whispered. "I
guess I do."

"Well, I want to know more about you, too. A lot
more," he replied with another heart-stopping smile.
Emory liked the way he touched her hand, lightly run-

ning his fingertips down the length of her own, savoring the touch of skin against skin, sending the oddest feathery sensation up and down her spine.

"You're hard to figure, Professor," he admitted.

"That's funny—I was just thinking the same about you, Detective," Emory replied with a teasing grin.

Before Nick could reply, their waiter had appeared and was suddenly bustling around the table, clearing their plates. Emory's dish was only half eaten. She had managed to eat the white rings of fish without much trouble, but hadn't been able to manage the tentacles that well, which the waiter immediately noticed.

"Something wrong with your dinner, Miss?" he asked with concern.

"Uh, no. It was delicious," she insisted.

"Shall I wrap this up for you to take home?" the waiter asked her.

"Uh, no, that's okay," Emory said, secretly glad to see it disappear into the kitchen.

Shaking his head in disapproval, the waiter handed the dishes to a nearby busboy. Nick looked over at her and laughed.

"It was very good," she insisted.

"If you like food that waves at you, you mean?" he said, cutting through her polite but transparent excuses. "I'll have to make it up to you some night with a bowl of my own spaghetti and meatballs," he promised. "A guaranteed all-time crowd pleaser."

"You've got a deal," Emory said, wondering if the event would ever come to pass.

On the ride back to Emory's apartment, she could not tell if the knot in her stomach was caused by her exotic dinner, Nick's driving, or the prospect of a good-night kiss from her handsome driver. As Nick chatted about the Babcock scheme, Emory mostly listened. Finally he pulled up to her doorstep.

"Thanks again for dinner," Emory said, her keys in hand. "I guess I'll call you as soon as I confirm a date with Babcock. Good night, Nick." Then she jumped out of the Jeep and slammed the door.

"I'll walk you to the door," Nick said, seemingly amused at her sudden nervousness. As he followed her up the front stairs, she realized she couldn't have moved any quicker if someone was chasing her.

At the front door she fumbled with the keys, hearing Nick's footsteps come closer and closer. Then he was standing right behind her, at the top of the steps, and his closeness made her even more distracted. "Damn...this key always sticks. I've spoken to the super about it," Emory rambled nervously, her key chain rattling.

"Here, let me try," Nick said, reaching out from behind her. Taking the keys from her hand, his chest was pressed to her back and he practically had both arms around her. Emory tried to keep looking straight ahead at the door.

"Hmm—it is tricky, isn't it?" Nick said after a moment.

"I don't know why we can't just get a new one. Everyone in the building complains about it—" She turned her head just the slightest bit in his direction, and then her body, so that they were standing face-to-face. Their eyes met in an instant and an instant later, Emory felt Nick's arms closing around her, pulling her close.

Nothing in his embrace asked permission, or offered any pretense, just as she would have predicted. Her eyes closed softly as their lips met, and she heard herself breathe his name on a sigh. His kiss began warm and slow, not tentatively but with an enticing pace. He seemed to be slowly savoring the first taste of her, as she had seen him savor the first sip of wine that night at dinner. He held her closer and closer, nearly lifting her up off her feet in his strong arms. This wasn't an ordinary good-night kiss... not the kind she was used to, anyway. This was a revelation, Emory thought in some distant, hazy part of her mind. What in the world had she been missing?

Emory wrapped her arms around his shoulders, parting her lips to meet the thrust of his tongue with her own. Engaged in an intimate dance of tasting, swirling, teasing each other, the nervousness she had felt in the Jeep was now suddenly transformed to an open, undisguised admission of her powerful attraction to him. As eager as she had been moments ago to hide safely behind her front door, she now felt a most compelling need to hold him even closer, their coats and clothes forcing an annoying interference to her pleasure.

Lost in a whirlpool of mindless sensation, Emory felt only the hard door behind her back and Nick's hard body molding with her own. Then a sudden mechanical pop sounded in her ear and she felt herself falling backward as the door swung open.

Luckily, Nick realized what was happening and tightened his hold on her. ''Well... we finally got that darned lock open,'' he said with a low laugh after a moment.

''Yes—I guess we did.'' She looked up at him then and took a deep breath. He was holding her by the shoulders now, not pushing her away exactly, but clearly not drawing her closer. When she looked into his eyes she saw the dark, smouldering light, but something else, as well. A look she could only describe as relief. Relief that they'd been so awkwardly called back to their senses? She felt breathless and shaky, wondering if she'd fall backward again when Nick finally let her go. Taking a cue from him, she stepped back, too, managing to at least look as if she could make it into her apartment under her own power without swooning at his feet.

"You won't have any trouble with your other door, will you?" Nick asked her politely.

"I think I can manage that one fine." Any thought that he expected to come in was quickly denied as he started down the steps.

"Good night, now," he called back over his shoulder.

"Good night, Nick," she said, feeling half relieved and half disappointed. He waved briefly as he got into his Jeep and she watched from the doorway as he pulled away and drove down the street.

Had it been her imagination, or had he seemed suddenly eager to get away from her? she wondered as she climbed up the stairs to her apartment. Emory still felt shaken from Nick's kiss, still in awe that a simple goodnight kiss could so swiftly...well, knock her socks off.

But perhaps the whole experience had been completely different for him, she thought then. Why else would he have tried to get away from her so quickly afterward? He was acting as if he'd suddenly realized the whole thing had been a mistake. There was no other way she could describe it. Emory felt her high-flying spirits come crashing down to earth. It made her feel even worse to realize that she hadn't held back at all, and had met his embrace so eagerly.

"Like the love-starved egghead he expects you to be," Emory chided herself as she flopped into bed. Leonardo hopped on the quilt, purring loudly and rubbing his furry head on her hand. Emory absent-mindedly petted him. I was about as subtle as good old Leonardo here, she said to herself, feeling embarrassed all over again.

Well, it wouldn't happen again, she promised herself. From now on she would hold herself in an even more businesslike manner. So she was attracted to him, well, so what? He certainly wasn't her type, today had proved that clearly enough. Teaching her how to eat spaghetti . . . The nerve of the man. The way he called out to the waiter to take their order. The man had no manners, no social skills whatsoever. Oh, there was always a certain amount of rough charm in that type, that was for sure. But it would wear on her nerves in no time, she reminded herself.

Even if his slightest kiss could make her feel as if she'd been sent straight into orbit. Emory turned over on her side and punched her pillow, trying not to think about that part. A fluke. A lucky shot. The wine and sheer novelty of it all. She'd have to watch herself in the future. She'd nearly made a big mistake tonight, thinking her attraction to the handsome detective could ever be anything more.

Four

Emory woke in a foul mood. Her earliest thoughts brought back the scene with Nick on her front doorstep. In the uncompromising light of day, it seemed even clearer that he had been relieved to escape from their embrace. She briefly considered backing out of her agreement to help him. But then she would have to face the wrath of the formidable Mrs. Newland. In a conversation last week, Mrs. Newland had made it clear that Emory's cooperation was expected without question. Emory knew her position as curator of the Newland collection might be in jeopardy if she dared to challenge this imperial "request" from her employer.

She would have to go through with it, that was clear. The best method for dealing with Detective Fiore was to act as if nothing had happened. *Less* than nothing, she promised herself.

Emory called Nolan Babcock from her office at the college that morning. Babcock recognized Emory's name immediately and also knew of her connection to Mrs. Newland. His unctuous manner practically oozed right through the phone line. She made the appointment for Friday afternoon, as Nick had instructed. Emory could swear her ear felt sticky when she finally hung up.

Her hand hovered over the phone buttons a moment as she next prepared to call Nick at the station house. Then she decided to take the coward's way out and leave a message on his answering machine at home, since she knew he wouldn't be there.

Even hearing his recorded greeting set off a confused flurry of feelings. She quickly left her message and hung up the phone, as if it were about to explode in her hand. She worried briefly about how she'd handle seeing him again on Friday. But that was four whole days away. By then she would barely remember a thing, she promised herself.

Teaching two classes, student appointments and a department meeting kept her busy all day and distracted from thoughts about Nick. That evening she had a dinner date with Cliff Lensky, a professor of European history. Another perfect distraction, she thought as she dressed.

Cliff took her to a quiet French café in Cambridge. It was a thoughtful choice, Emory realized, since she'd only mentioned it once as one of her favorites. It was their first real date and he was obviously eager to please her. Unfortunately, as the evening wore on, practically everything Cliff did to impress her turned out to have the opposite effect. Emory couldn't quite understand it.

Tall and thin, with blond hair and a beard, she had always thought Cliff quite attractive. She had wanted him to ask her out for a long time. For some inexplicable reason, as she gazed across the candlelight at him, the dashing young upstart of the history department looked...well, sort of bland to her tonight. His tweed sport coat, woolen vest and sedate tie actually looked drab. As drab as his conversation about the influence of Spanish monarchs on the Dutch Masters. The topic would have normally enthralled her, but tonight the conversation left Emory fighting a strong urge to yawn.

She was, of course, comparing the poor man to Nick. Even the careful, cautious way he drove his Volvo got on her nerves. Unfair, Emory, she secretly scolded herself. Give the poor man a break. Just as Nick had, Cliff dutifully followed her up the front steps to her door. Unlike Nick, however, he waited a step or two below, careful not to crowd her.

The finicky lock snapped open on the first try and she turned to Cliff with a wide smile of relief. "Well, thanks again for a lovely evening."

"My pleasure," he said. "Do you have any plans for the weekend? There's a terrific movie playing at the Metro," he said, mentioning a movie house in Cambridge that featured foreign films.

"I'll be in New York this weekend," she said, hoping to feign an appropriate note of regret in her voice.

"Oh, really? How nice for you. Visiting friends?" he asked.

He really wanted to know if she was going to visit some other man, she guessed. "Uh—no. Not at all. It's just business."

"Oh, well. Hope it's interesting business," he said cheerfully.

Emory thought then of Nick, who frankly had not been that far from her thoughts all evening. "It should be interesting," she said.

"Have a good trip. I'll call you next week sometime, okay?"

"I'd like that," Emory forced herself to say. Sure, she'd had a completely lackluster date with the man, but on some level she knew he was a good and suitable choice for her, like eating more fiber. As opposed to Nick, who was more like a steady diet of pizza and hot fudge sundaes.

Encouraged by her reply, Cliff took that important step up to where they were eye level. He leaned over and quickly kissed her on the lips. It was not the type of kiss that required a response, or even gave her time to respond if she had wanted to. Again, quite unlike the way Nick had ended their evening. Greatly relieved, she said good-night again, went inside and closed the door.

The counter on her answering machine showed the number one. One guess who that is, Emory said to herself as she pushed the playback button.

"Nick Fiore returning your call—" the message began. Nick *Fiore*, Emory fumed. How dare he kiss her like that, then leave his last name, as if they were barely acquainted!

"—Glad to hear the appointment with Babcock is set. I'll pick you up at nine Friday morning for the airport. I've taken care of the hotel arrangements. If you have any questions, give me a call. Otherwise, see you then. Have a good week, Professor."

"Stop calling me that!" Emory grumbled out loud as the machine clicked off. "It's *really* getting on my nerves."

* * *

The week passed quickly. Emory's Friday schedule
was light, so it was an easy day to take off. At precisely five minutes to nine, she stood on the sidewalk
outside her building. She was wearing her New York
outfit—a pencil-thin black skirt that fell to her mid-calf
and black, three-quarter-length blazer, tailored to her
slim body with asymmetrical buttons. The weather was
mild, even for early April. Instead of a coat, she chose
a large, thin wool stole, with a swirling paisley pattern
in purple, amber, black and green. She wrapped it in a
fashionable twist across her shoulders. With a large-
brimmed black felt hat and sunglasses, her hair up in
an elegant twist, she felt armed and ready for the
Manhattan art scene.

Nick's black Jeep roared down her street a few minutes later, lurching to a stop at the curb where she
stood. Nick hopped out and greeted her with a bright
smile.

"My, my...I almost didn't recognize you," he said,
making her feel self-conscious with his appraising stare.
"The Mata Hari look suits you," he added, taking her
carry-on bag and tossing it into the Jeep's back seat.

Emory preferred to ignore his fashion critique. Mata
Hari, indeed. The man had no fashion sense whatsoever. The dark blue suit he wore had the cut of a large
cardboard box and looked like he probably pulled it
out about twice a year—for weddings and funerals, she
guessed. Babcock was going to think Nick was an insurance salesman. Well, she couldn't worry about it.
Why he still looked so darned good in the awful suit
was a mystery to her, however.

"Good morning," she said simply. Getting into the
Jeep in her narrow skirt and high heels while preserv-

ing some shred of dignity required some surprising gymnastics. Nick seemed to be thoroughly enjoying the performance.

"Nice day for flying," she said inanely, hoping to distract him.

"Not a cloud in the sky," he commented dryly, his gaze lingering on her legs.

"No, not a cloud. They say it will be fair right through the weekend, too." There, weather was always a safe topic. She had even brought work along with her so that she'd have an easy way to avoid socializing with him. To act any other way was only asking for trouble. He'd surely get the message soon enough.

Nick gave her a curious glance, but didn't say anything more as he deftly maneuvered the Jeep through the rush-hour traffic. They were soon at Logan airport. He let Emory off with the bags and parked the Jeep in a short-term lot. They met at the shuttle gate and were lucky enough to get seats on a flight that was just boarding.

As soon as they were buckled in and the plane began its taxi down the runway, Emory took out an art magazine and a big sheaf of student papers from her briefcase. Barely casting Nick a glance, she picked up a paper and began reading.

"So, are you nervous?" Nick asked her once the plane had taken off.

"Nervous? No, I don't think so. I think it will go all right," Emory replied.

"It'll go just fine," Nick said reassuringly. "I just thought you might be having a few second thoughts... this being your first undercover operation and all."

An interesting choice of words, Emory reflected. Was she actually going undercover with Nick, in a manner of speaking? Then she did have good cause for an attack of nerves.

"I'm not having any second thoughts," Emory said evenly, jotting red marks in the margin of the paper in her hand. "Are you nervous?" she challenged him.

"Me? Maybe not nervous, exactly. A little psyched up, you might say. It's hard for me to sit still like this for too long." He leaned back in his seat, and squirmed a bit. He was obviously too active to sit quietly even for a short flight.

"I'll tell you what makes me nervous," he said then.

"What?" Emory finally looked up at him.

"Talking to someone wearing sunglasses," he said pointedly.

"Oh, sorry—" She slipped off her glasses. It was rude of her, she knew. But she felt somehow protected from him behind them. When they were off, she felt suddenly exposed. "My eyes felt a little sensitive to light this morning. Grading too many papers last night, I guess."

She smiled, then scribbled a grade at the top of the sheet, and turned to the next in the stack.

"Not all, I see." Emory did not look up, barely murmuring in response.

"I'll bet you're a hard marker," he persisted. "Don't give out many A's, right?"

"What makes you think that?" she replied with a laugh.

"It just figures," he said with a shrug. "I'm right, aren't I?"

"Sort of," she replied, not willing for some reason to admit that she was indeed quite stingy with her A's.

"I used to love teachers like you in college," he said with a reminiscent sigh to his voice. "I bet I could have gotten an A out of you."

"Oh, really?" Emory finally looked up at him, her voice clearly denoted her disbelief. "You have some secret formula?"

"Wouldn't you like to know? I bet I could have," he said again, sounding quite sure of himself. "You know there's two kinds of smart, Professor," he added. "You're one kind."

"—And you're the other?" she finished for him.

"Sort of." He nodded. He folded his arms across his chest and leaned back in his seat. "It's a good combination. I've been thinking about it," he admitted.

It was an act of will for Emory not to look back up at him then and acknowledge his admission. She could feel Nick's dark gaze on her as he waited for some response. But somehow she managed to feign concentration on her papers.

Nick was quiet for a few minutes, fidgeting in his seat he began bobbing his knee. He was like a little boy on a car trip, Emory thought, secretly smiling to herself. Any minute she expected him to ask her, "Aren't we there *yet?*" Finally he reached into his carry-on bag and pulled out a book. Emory snuck a glance at the title, *Elvis: The Legend Lives On.*

Nick caught her looking. "Investigative reporting," he said defensively. "About, uh, Elvis's ghost. It's really fascinating."

"Really? Any pictures?" Emory asked dryly.

"It came with a poster. Glows in the dark," he replied with a devilish grin.

LaGuardia airport was crowded and hectic and Emory was secretly thankful for the way Nick strong-armed them through the crowd and into a waiting limo near the cabstand, where a driver stood holding a small white card that said Fiore. "Manhattan," he called to the driver from the back seat. "The Plaza."

"The *Plaza?*" Emory echoed.

"Hey—you're traveling with the Boston P.D. Class act all the way," he said smoothly. "Where did you think I'd book us, at the Roadside Hideaway?"

"No—but the Plaza . . ."

"We have to maintain our cover," he reminded her. "Besides, I bet you stay in those fancy hotels all the time. This isn't going to be any big change for you, Professor," he said, sounding so sure the comment did not require a response. "And for me . . . well, on a case like this they expect you to take a few perks. I really love those big towels at the good places," he added as he began to explore the limo's luxury back seat features. Like a kid opening a big Christmas present, Emory thought. "You know, those kinds of towels that are about four inches thick and wrap around you about five times? I love that."

"I know the kind you mean," Emory said, avoiding his gaze as she fitted her sunglasses into her purse. The vision of Nick wrapping his naked, shower-fresh body in a huge towel gave Emory a sudden rush of warmth. Okay, she was still allowed a fantasy or two, wasn't she? As long as it didn't go any further, she reminded herself.

Nick was busily pulling open doors in the console to find a miniature TV, CD player and a fully stocked liquor cabinet. "Now this is my idea of riding in style. Can I fix you a cold drink? A mineral water, perhaps? We seem to have your favorite brand."

How did he know it was her favorite brand? He must have taken notice at her apartment on Saturday afternoon. He was a detective, Emory reminded herself. "Thanks," she said, taking the cut-crystal glass from his hand. It even had ice cubes and a twist of lemon.

"For *moi*," he said in an exaggerated French accent, "the vintage diet cola." Nick poured himself a drink and took a sip. "Ah, perfectly chilled."

"You really are enjoying this, aren't you?" Emory asked with a small smile.

"Hey, what can I say? It's a dirty job—"

"—but somebody's got to do it?" she finished for him.

"Wow! A Yankee-Red Sox game!" he replied, totally distracted by the TV. With a grin that stretched from ear to ear, Nick leaned back and stretched out. "How lucky can a guy get? All we need now is a pizza," he said with a sigh, loosening his tie.

"Why don't you call out for one? Maybe you could get a delivery to meet you at the Triboro Bridge."

"Good idea," Nick said, totally oblivious to her sarcasm. He picked up the phone. "What do you like on it?"

"This is going to be an experience." Emory sighed to herself as she slipped her glasses back on and turned to stare out the window. How had he turned into a tycoon, right before her very eyes? Was it something in the limo's air-conditioning?

"Professor, the fun has just begun," he promised her.

Much to his disappointment, Nick was not able to order a pizza delivery at the Triboro Bridge from the car phone. However, once their limousine reached midtown, he did request frequent stops at the pushcart food vendors he spotted all along Central Park. By the time they reached the hotel he'd managed to consume a shish kebab sandwich, two hot dogs and half a bag of roasted macadamia nuts.

When they checked in, she was relieved to hear that their rooms were on different floors. Then she chided herself for being silly. What had she feared? The makings of a romantic, hotel room farce, á la Rock Hudson, Doris Day? She'd once read that secret fears are really wishes turned inside out. As Emory signed her check-in card and collected her key, she pushed the niggling thought aside.

"Our appointment with Babcock isn't until three," Nick said, glancing at his watch as they waited for the elevator. "What should we do until then?"

"I have to visit a gallery downtown, in Soho," Emory informed him crisply. "I should be back by about two-thirty."

The business she planned to conduct in Soho could have easily been handled by phone, but she had promised herself to pull out every rabbit in her Mata Hari hat to keep Nick at arm's length during this trip.

The elevator arrived and they squeezed in with a large group of hotel guests. Emory was forced to stand uncomfortably close beside Nick.

"Soho, huh? Maybe I should come with you. Lots of weirdos down there," he replied as the doors closed.

"I think I can manage, thanks. I've traveled to New York before without a bodyguard."

"I'm sure that's true. But I do have a professional duty to keep close watch on *your* body, Professor," he said slyly. "Not that I'm complaining by any stretch of the imagination," he assured her with a slow appraising gaze at her figure.

"You're pushing your luck, Nick," Emory said crisply.

"It's true. Without you this whole case is down the tubes."

"So that means you more or less will follow me around the city all day...like...like a guard dog or something?" Emory asked with an exasperated sigh.

She turned toward him and looked up. His face was close to hers, she might have leaned up on tiptoe with no problem at all for their lips to meet. He was smiling down at her, a dancing light in his eyes, amused by her annoyance, which made her even more annoyed.

"In a word...woof..." He leaned over and licked her lightly on the cheek. "Don't worry, I'm house-broken," he whispered in a taunting manner.

"Down boy," she whispered in a low but firm tone.

Nick lifted his head, startled at first by the remark. Then, laughing quietly, he backed a respectable distance away.

"I'd better watch it. Next thing I know, you'll be swatting my nose with a rolled-up newspaper."

"I might...but I'm not sure it would help." The doors opened to her floor and she stepped out. "I'll meet you in the lobby in fifteen minutes."

Five

They had begun their walk in Soho by stopping in some of the galleries Emory worked with, and some that were new. Nick was a quiet shadow most of the time, soaking up the conversation in preparation for the meeting with Babcock. He didn't seem to have much interest in anything hanging on the gallery walls. He was totally fascinated however by the sights outside the galleries, the crowds that filled the narrow winding streets below Houston Street in the city's "hippest" neighborhood.

"The way these kids dress around here! I mean, I thought I'd seen it all in Boston, but these kids look like they've just landed from another planet."

"They would probably say the same about you," Emory observed, once again appraising his suit, possibly the blandest-looking piece of clothing on the eastern seaboard, she decided.

Nick looked at her, and then down at his clothes. "What's wrong with the way I'm dressed? It's a regular, old blue suit," he replied indignantly.

"*Definitely* old and *extremely* regular," Emory replied with a thin smile. "Nolan Babcock is going to think you're selling insurance."

"Very funny. Maybe I should get a flat-top haircut and wear a black leather dog collar around my neck. I'd fit right in with that hipper-than-thou look around here," he said, gesturing to the young crowd that milled past them on lower Broadway.

"I don't know about the haircut, but the dog collar would be some improvement over that tie," Emory said bluntly with a sweet smile.

"Now it's the tie, too?" He picked up his tie and looked at it, shaking his head. "What's wrong with this tie? It's your basic goes-anywhere type of neckwear."

"It's basic all right. I'll grant you that much," Emory replied, deciding now to hold nothing back. As he re-examined his tie however, she had to smile at the dismayed expression on his handsome face.

Quite coincidentally, their fashion debate had brought them to a spot on lower Broadway that was an open-air flea market. Vendors with folding tables sold everything from tape cassettes to underwear—hats, costume jewelry, ties, sunglasses, shirts, even racks of antique clothes and the hipper-than-thou outfits Nick had earlier referred to, in Spandex, leather and other trendy fabrics.

"Here—why don't you try one of these ties?" Emory suggested, sifting through a nearby rack of wide silk ties with wild floral patterns or nineteen forty-ish, art deco designs. She finally settled on one with black, gold and small "retro" style palm trees.

"It will ruin my appetite—" Nick complained as he held the tie up to his chest and peered into a small mirror.

"I sincerely doubt anything could do that," Emory said, peering at him from over the top of her sunglasses, which had slid down the bridge of her nose.

"You really *like* this tie? Better than this nice striped one?" he replied, ignoring her barb.

"In a word...unquestionably." Emory knew the time was now or never to snatch away the offensive, natty neckwear in exchange for her selection. "Besides, we have to remember your cover story."

"Right," Nick said reluctantly as he tied the tie on. When he started to pay the vendor, Emory had already taken care of it. "My treat," she said graciously.

"Thanks." He looked a little mollified by her gesture. Not much, but a little.

"Now, how about one of these jackets...or leather vests?" she suggested as they moved to the next set of stalls. "But you'll need a new shirt to pull it all together," she added, her hand running along a pile of interesting-looking men's shirts. "This mustard-colored one is great looking. He'd like to try that one on," Emory told the vendor.

"Hey—just a second. The cover story is that I'm your assistant—not your latest redecorating project!"

"What size are you, a medium?" Emory asked, ignoring his fussing. This was actually turning out to be fun. From the moment she'd seen him in that suit this morning, she'd been dying to "redecorate" him...if the truth be told.

"I'm a *large*," he said proudly. "I have very wide shoulders."

"Can we see this in a large, please?" Emory said sweetly to the young man in black leather behind the table.

"We're *just* looking...honestly," Nick said to the vendor, who was by now thoroughly confused.

The afternoon flew by as Nick and Emory continued shopping and haggling with each other. They suddenly realized it was time for a quick stop at their hotel before their meeting with Babcock.

"I look like I'm on my way to a Halloween party," Nick complained, stretching his neck to get a better look at himself in the cab's rearview mirror. "I can't believe I let you talk me into dressing up like this. I must be out of my mind. If anybody from the force ever saw me like this, they'd have me committed."

"I think you look very nice," Emory replied simply. The new and improved Nick looked impossibly cute in his "arty" look, Emory thought. In addition to the tie, he was wearing the mustard-colored linen shirt and had exchanged his suit jacket for a leather jacket, which Emory sparked with a silver pin shaped like a lightning bolt.

"Those palm trees do wonders for your eyes." She knew it was risky to tease him at such lengths, but she honestly couldn't resist.

"Wonders for my eyes, huh?" he echoed in disbelief. "You expect me to buy that?" he challenged her.

"Don't believe me." She shrugged, hiding a smile. Something in his eyes told her that a very small, secret part of him did believe her.

Besides, he had gotten back at her in his way. He had insisted they could not leave the clothes stalls before he picked out some outrageous piece of clothing he wanted her to wear. Emory had first tried to talk him out of it, but saw that he meant his word. She did want to be fair. She held her breath as he made his selection. He spent an inordinate amount of time at the satin and leather bustier table. Fair was one thing, but she wasn't going to dress up like a rock and roll queen! Not for a million dollars.

To her relative relief, he finally came up with a black leather miniskirt. Not so daring by Soho standards, but certainly enough on the wild side for Emory.

"And that skirt does wonders for your legs," he said, casting a long lingering glance at her legs. Emory shifted restlessly, feeling as if her entire body was exposed to his savoring appraisal. But unfortunately, stuck in the back of the cab, with the skirt edging up slowly to her throat, there was little she could do to cover more of her.

Emory was relieved when the taxi pulled up to their destination. As Nick paid the driver, she tried to wriggle out of the cab preserving as much of her dignity as possible. The gallery was in a brownstone on the upper east side, not far from the Metropolitan Museum of Art. As they approached a gallery assistant, Emory whispered to Nick, "I think you'd better let me do most of the talking."

"I've been letting you do *all* of the talking *all* day," he grumbled. "Look where it's gotten me...dressed up like an escapee from a music video...." His voice trailed off to a sudden attack of throat clearing, his frown instantly replaced by a silly looking grin.

"May I help you?" the gallery attendant asked Nick politely. She was a tall, thin, pretty redhead in her early twenties, wearing a red cashmere turtleneck, and of all things, a black leather miniskirt, black stockings and flats. Maybe Nick's taste wasn't so bad after all, Emory thought.

"We have an appointment with Mr. Babcock," Emory said. "Emory Byrd...and my associate..." Emory paused, thinking suddenly that perhaps Nick didn't want her to use his real name. What if Nolan Babcock was smarter than Nick thought? He might be suspicious enough to check up on Nick and find out he was a cop. No, better to think up some alias, Emory decided in a panicky split second. "Oliver Brisbain."

Luckily, Nick was standing behind the gallery attendant and she could not see the dumbfounded look on his face.

"I'll tell him you're here," the young woman said politely. "Would you like some coffee, or a cold drink?"

"Uh, no thanks," Emory said, forcing a smile. "We'll just look around a bit." She took Nick's arm and steered him toward some paintings on the opposite wall.

"Oliver Brisbain?" he rasped under his breath.

"I didn't want Babcock to trace your real name. He might have connections you're unaware of, you know," Emory hissed back.

"I suppose that's possible," Nick said, taking her point into consideration. "But how did you ever arrive at—"

"Oliver Brisbain is one of my graduate students who's had some articles published on South American surrealists," Emory cut in sharply. "If Babcock recognizes the name, he won't be suspicious."

"Good idea," Nick grumbled begrudgingly. "Just my luck that your smartest student couldn't have a real name, like, say, Jack or Joe—"

Their whispered argument was interrupted by the sight of a tall, silver-haired man walking across the gallery toward them. He was dressed in an elegant olive green linen suit and a tan shirt of some expensive-looking fabric. His tie, made from hand-painted silk, was itself suitable for framing on the gallery walls, as well. Emory presumed he was Nolan Babcock.

"Hush—here he comes," she reprimanded Nick.

"Ms. Byrd?" Nolan Babcock extended his hand toward her. "How wonderful to finally meet you. I was so pleased when you called us the other day."

"It's nice of you to make time to see us, Mr. Babcock," Emory said. "This is my associate, Oliver Brisbain."

"Mr. Brisbain." Nolan politely shook Nick's hand in greeting. "Haven't we met before?" he asked Nick. "Last year in London? Your name does ring a bell."

"Perhaps," Nick said with a slight nod of his head.

"We were just enjoying this exhibit," Emory cut in, trying to divert the conversation away from Nick. "Are these recent works from Salazar? I heard she was moving into larger canvases."

Babcock quickly launched into a detailed update on his featured artist. Ninety percent of the conversation, she guessed, was breezing by Nick as if they were speaking a foreign language. She hoped that Babcock—who seemed very pleased to hear himself talk—would not notice her "assistant's" uncharacteristic shyness.

"So, Mrs. Newland has developed an interest in South American surrealists? A new phase for her, isn't it?"

"Uh, no. Her latest phase is actually Australian counterclockwise expressionism," Nick replied with a serious expression.

"Counterclockwise . . . expressionism?" Babcock said, looking thoroughly perplexed.

"Well, of course you realize that below the equator, everything turns backward. For example, our summer is their winter. Water going down the drain turns counterclockwise, too," Nick added, as if that explained everything. "They have a different artistic perspective down there, naturally. The expression of their proximity to . . . the South Pole, I suppose."

"Yes . . . of course," Babcock replied, eyeing Nick quizzically. He then turned to Emory, his expression once again under control. "I believe I read something about this only recently. The use of many primitive, Aborigine symbols incorporated in a post-modern sensibility?"

"That's it exactly," Emory replied quickly. She was beginning to feel like Alice in Wonderland. All Nick's fault, of course. He was merely mimicking all the conversations he'd overheard today in the downtown galleries. She supposed he thought he was being supremely clever. She only hoped Babcock wasn't suspicious.

"It's really *Ollie's* area of *expertise,*" she said, throwing Nick a poisonous glance. "Sometimes, even I don't know what he's talking about." She laughed nervously. Discreetly prodding Nick with her elbow, he began laughing then, too.

Hoping to join in the "joke" Nolan Babcock began laughing also, his quizzical expression suggesting to Emory that he had no idea of what he was laughing at. Anything for a sale though, she was sure.

"Let's move into the next room, shall we?" Nolan said smoothly, guiding Emory by the arm. "I'd like to show you an absolutely stunning piece by a new sculptor I've just begun to represent. He works mostly in compressed soda cans. Very exciting vision. I'm sure you'll appreciate it, Emory."

As the tour continued into the next room, Nick decided to take his cues from Emory and hung back. That elbow jab she'd given him had qualified as an assault with a deadly weapon, he thought as he rubbed the sore spot below a rib. But she was right. He'd nearly blown it with his counterclockwise claptrap. She'd kept her cool, though. He had to grant her that. She was really amazingly good at this. A born con artist, he decided with a secret grin. Her pedigree packaging could camouflage a lot. She was something else, this Professor Emory Byrd, Nick thought as he observed her with Babcock in the next room, circling a sculpture that looked like the bottom of a recycling bin. There was more to this woman than met the eye, that was for sure. He'd been learning that lesson at every turn since they'd met.

As for Nolan Babcock, well he was about as genuine as one of those Rolex watches sold by street peddlers. Nick had figured Babcock out from across the room. One look at that slicked-back silver hair and custom-made suit was all he needed. Babcock was totally ignoring him now, but pouring on the charm in Emory's direction. Did he have to stand so close to her while they looked over that junk heap sculpture? These slimy, touchy-feely gallery owners probably came on to her all the time. She seemed to be handling it fine. But that didn't mean he had to like it.

Nick sighed. His strong surge of jealousy and possessiveness about Emory surprised him. Hold on, pal, he chided himself, this woman is really getting to you.

As Babcock touched Emory's shoulder to direct attention to another piece, Nick felt his temper rising. Then realized he was about to interrupt with some outrageously ignorant remark and ruin the whole setup. Let the clever professor get the job done on her own, she doesn't need your help, he decided. Besides, he could take the time to get a good look around without dear old Nolan looking over his shoulder.

"I don't know much about the Newland collection, I must confess," Babcock said to Emory as they stood before the last painting in the room. "Aside from her new interest in surrealists... and that Australian movement, of course. Is Mrs. Newland looking for anything in particular? Works from any particular painter or school?"

"Works from any particular painter?" Emory echoed. Wasn't this the perfect cue? The perfect moment to bring up Truffaut? It was happening exactly as Nick had explained it. Yet when she turned to see how her "assistant" would reply, he was gone!

"Mrs. Newland has many areas of interest. The collection is quite wide-ranging," Emory began, clasping her sweaty palms. She looked around for Nick, but he was nowhere to be seen.

"Yes, of course. I would imagine that's true," Babcock drawled. "Unlike some, who seem ... well, practically obsessed with one period. Or even one artist," he added.

"Well, to be perfectly honest..." Emory paused and decided to simply plunge right in. Her voice dropped to a low, confidential tone. "She does have an obsession with a certain artist. I suppose there's no other way to describe it.''

"Really?" Babcock replied in a gossipy, "girl-friend" tone. "The poor dear. These secret passions can drive a person mad, they say," he quipped.

"Her desire for more work by Truffaut may have to drive her mad," Emory said, relieved to finally fit in the painter's name. "We've managed to acquire a painting or two, a bronze figure. Of course, she'd like more—"

"Of course," Babcock cut in, in a sympathetic tone.

"—But there's so little of his work available."

"How true," Babcock nodded and sighed. His long fingers nervously smoothed his silk tie. Emory could almost hear the switches flipping behind his patrician forehead.

Emory turned away from Nolan Babcock, pretending to be interested in a mobile that jutted out from the wall. She did not want his cold blue eyes staring into hers. She was afraid of what he might see there. Where in the world had Nick gotten to? She was almost afraid to be alone with Babcock in this secluded back room. She had the instinctive feeling his polished veneer hid a desperate soul.

"Whenever one talks of Truffaut these days, one can't help but wonder about the *Blue Vase with Yellow Tulips*. Where it might be now, I mean," Babcock said, coming up behind her. Uncomfortably close, she thought. "Perhaps some collector is enjoying it, privately. Maybe even . . . Mrs. Newland," he ventured to add with an easy laugh.

"I only wish that were true. It would probably make my life a great deal easier," Emory laughed.

Calm down, she coached herself. No need for over-kill. The man has certainly gotten the message by now. She only hoped she could remember the conversation, word for word, when it came time to recollect it for Nick's benefit. Where was Nick?

"Would it really?" Babcock asked thoughtfully. "Well, perhaps your wish will be granted someday. Stranger things have happened, I suspect," he said in an offhand manner.

The look in his eyes made Emory profoundly nervous. She had seen that look before—particularly from her department chairman during faculty cocktail parties. Luckily, they had already begun walking back in the direction of the larger, first gallery.

"A few of the works in this room interest me," Emory said abruptly. "I'll discuss them with Mrs. Newland."

"Of course. I've prepared a packet for you—some slides, the catalog and some other materials," he said, walking off in the direction of his office. "I'll only be a minute. Why don't you let Bettina fix you a coffee?"

"That would be nice." Emory turned to look for the gallery attendant and then spotted her in a far corner. Busily serving Nick, she hardly noticed Emory's approach. Nick sat on a small marble bench, sipping a cup of espresso, a plate of exquisite-looking canapés balanced on his knee.

"Blini," he said, pointing down to a tiny pancake stuffed with caviar and sour cream. "I got some caviar on my tie, but you can hardly see it. Blends right in," Nick said brightly.

In a sweeping glance, Emory took in the cozy scene and the chagrined expression on Nick's face. She was fuming. This guy had some nerve, taking high tea with Little Miss Muffet here, while she was playing footsie with the Big Black Spider in the next room. And all for the greater glory of *his* police department! Well, he'd get an earful in the cab ride back to the hotel, that was for sure.

"And I thought caviar was on the endangered hors d'oeuvre list," Emory said wryly.

"Is it really?" Bettina sounded sincerely concerned.

"Well, that does it for me. I'm stuffed." Nick patted his mouth with a small cocktail napkin as he read the ire in Emory's amber eyes.

"Will wonders ever cease?" Emory said with poisonous sweetness.

"Here you go," Babcock said, joining them. He handed Emory a large manila envelope that looked as if it might contain a copy of the Manhattan Yellow Pages. "I'm so pleased you thought of us," he practically purred as he shook her hand goodbye. "I have a feeling the Newland collection will benefit tremendously from our future association."

"I hope so," Emory said, finally managing to extract her hand from his.

"Nice to meet you, Nolan," Nick said with a nonchalant nod.

"A pleasure to meet you, Oliver," Nolan replied smoothly.

"Nice space you've got here. Lots of light... Oh, and the refreshments were top rate, really," Nick effused.

"I'm so glad you enjoyed them," Nolan replied. "Goodbye for now," he said to Emory again, a puzzled expression on his face.

Six

Rush-hour traffic made it difficult to find a cab when they left the gallery. Emory suggested that they start walking down Fifth Avenue along Central Park. She had a lot of energy to burn up after her first "undercover" episode. She was also angry at Nick.

"Would you mind carrying this?" she said to Nick as she handed him the huge envelope from Babcock. Accidentally on purpose, she quite nearly landed a low punch to his middle with the package. "It's quite heavy," she warned him a second too late.

"Ugh—so it is." Nick drew in a pained breath. "No problem," he said, quickening his pace to keep up with her. "Hey, slow down. What's the rush?"

"Walking too fast for you? Maybe your snack made you sluggish."

"Oh, is that what's bugging you? Caught me 'snacking' on the job?"

"I thought you were going to help me with Babcock," Emory complained. "I mean, what do I know about this sort of thing? I could have messed up entirely. You said you were going to be there, every step of the way. And the minute I turn around, you vanish into thin air... No, make that a plate of blini."

Served with a side order of miniskirted French pastry, she added silently.

"You asked me to let you do all the talking, so I did," Nick defended himself. "Besides, the minute we got in there I could tell you had Babcock in the palm of your hand. I was only cramping your style, Mata Hari."

"Cramping my style? You nearly blew the whole plan with that ridiculous line about...counterclockwise expressionism. Whatever possessed you?"

"You didn't like that line?" Nick sounded genuinely surprised. "I thought that was pretty good. Bettina was enthralled."

"Yes, well, I don't doubt it. She didn't exactly strike me as the intellectual type," Emory said in a haughty tone.

"Now, now, Professor," Nick laughed. "I thought she might know something about the painting. I was trying to get a little information out of her. Anyone would think that you were...well, jealous."

"Hardly!" Emory fumed, the accusation making her only madder because she knew, in truth, that he was right. But she'd rather throw herself in front of the oncoming traffic on Fifth Avenue than admit it.

"You could have helped more with Babcock," she said once again. "Maybe I didn't even say the right thing to him when he brought up the painting."

"You talked about the painting with him?" Nick stopped walking and turned to her. "Why didn't you say so in the first place? Go on, let's hear a full report, word by word."

"I think I can remember it all. I know for sure that he mentioned the painting first," Emory replied, unable to hide her excitement.

She went on to relate her entire conversation with Babcock. She tried to remember every word, knowing it all might be important.

"I honestly had the feeling he was hinting about the possibility that Mrs. Newland might want to buy it, as you said he might," she concluded.

"I think you're right," Nick said, seemingly elated at their progress. "The guy is rolling over for us. It's too good to be true," he said cheerfully. "You handled yourself like a pro in there," he congratulated her.

"Oh... I just did what you told me. It wasn't very difficult," Emory replied.

"The hell it wasn't. That guy is crafty. No doubt about it. But you handled him just right. You were great." Nick flung his arm around her shoulder and gave her a comradely squeeze of affection. "Brilliant, in fact. I knew you would be," Nick added, turning to her.

The warm look in his eyes was almost more than Emory could handle. She swiftly and completely forgot her earlier moment of annoyance with him. The feeling of Nick's body close to hers as they strolled along the park, their steps finally in the same rhythm, made her forget almost everything.

"What do we do next?" Emory asked. "About Babcock, I mean."

"We wait. If he really does have the painting, he'll make the next move," Nick said confidently. "Does he know how to reach you?"

"I believe I mentioned to him that we were staying at the Plaza."

"Good. I think we should hang around until tomorrow, in case he decides to move quickly. And you know what that means," he added.

"No...what?" Emory asked, her voice coming out a bit squeaky. She hoped he hadn't noticed.

"With any luck I can pick up some tickets for the play-off game down at Madison Square Garden," he replied excitedly, as if announcing that the mayor had invited him to dine at Gracie Mansion.

"The play-off game? What exactly is being...played off?" Emory asked him, being totally ignorant about sports. She didn't even know what season it was. Hadn't he just been watching a baseball game in the car?

"Hoops. Basketball. The NBA championship," he replied, dumbfounded at her ignorance. "Followed by a major steak at Gallaghers... No! I've got it." He snapped his fingers, gripped by a sudden inspiration. "A hot pastrami sandwich at Second Avenue Deli."

As Nick mused over his dinner menu, Emory suddenly realized that she was clearly not included in these plans. She felt hurt. It was jarring after the closeness they'd shared all day. But Nick's snub—intentional or not—only served to remind her that she had promised herself she would keep a safe distance from him.

"I—uh—have some plans, too," she said finally.

"You do?" The tone of his voice made Emory think suddenly that she had been mistaken. Maybe he had intended to include her in his hoops—and—hot pastrami plans. Too late now, she decided.

"Yes, I do. Some friends in the city who I don't see often have invited me out to dinner," she explained lightly. The invitation was one of the open-ended sort and Emory still had to call to confirm. But Nick needn't know that she'd been leaving her night flexible on the chance he might ask her to join him. "Bibi and I went to college together. Her husband, Charles, works for the Met, so we have a lot to talk about."

"Really? I didn't know you liked baseball, Professor," Nick said, looking at her with renewed interest.

"Baseball? What does baseball have to do with the Metropolitan Museum of Art?" Emory asked, looking at him with a puzzled expression.

"Oh...you meant..." Nick shook his head. "I thought you said he worked for the *Mets*. The baseball team?" he asked her.

"Oh...no. Sorry," Emory said, though she didn't quite know why she was apologizing. Another miscommunication with Nick. She was almost getting used to these weird conversations. The thought was a bit frightening.

"Never mind." They'd arrived at the hotel and the doorman held open the door for them as they walked into the lobby. "Well, have fun with your friends," he said abruptly.

"Thank you," Emory said, feeling puzzled at his reaction. "Have fun at the basketball game."

"You bet," Nick said with a curt nod. "See you later." He walked off in the direction of the hotel shops.

When Emory reached her room, she felt suddenly drained. She stepped out of her shoes, tossed her purse and scarf on the dresser. Then undressed down to her slip and stockings before lying down on the bed. It had been a long day. She felt as if she'd left Nick on a bad note. But that couldn't be helped, she reminded herself. She could admit, at least to herself, that she'd wanted him to ask her to the basketball game. But he hadn't. It was just as well.

The phone rang and Emory sat up to answer it. Was it Nick, calling with a last minute invitation? "Emory? Hi, it's Bibi—" a familiar voice said.

"Bibi—I just got in the room this minute. Sorry I haven't had a chance to call you all day. What time shall I come by tonight?"

"Oh, Emory, I'm so sorry. That's just why I was calling. We have a little problem with dinner tonight—" Bibi went on to explain that her three-year-old twins were both sick with the flu and she wouldn't dream of leaving them with a sitter. "I'd invite you here, but the place is really upside down and I wouldn't want you to catch anything."

"Please, don't worry about it. It sounds like you and Charles have your hands full tonight," Emory said sincerely. "I'll find some way to amuse myself."

"Thanks for being such a good sport about it," Bibi said, sounding relieved. "I knew you'd understand."

Emory *despised* doing things alone, *especially* on a Friday night in a big city like New York. But she didn't want her friend to know that. She and Bibi chatted for a while, and then made plans to get together in a few weeks, when the couple would be up in Boston.

Emory lay back on the bed, looking up at the ceiling. She had two choices. She could either stay in her room and mark papers all night...and brood about Nick. Or she could take advantage of a night in New

York City and treat herself to a special night out. A reward, she decided, for keeping her promise and keeping Nick at a safe distance. A reward ... or a cold comfort? Well, what did it matter? Emory thought, springing up from the bed. She couldn't sit up here all night, that was for sure. She'd go crazy.

She dialed the entertainment desk in the hotel lobby. "May I help you?" a young man asked her.

"Uh, yes, I'd like a ticket for tonight's performance at the Metropolitan Opera."

"Just one?" he asked her.

"Uh, yes. One," Emory repeated. It was one of those moments when the world reminded her of just how *extremely* single she really was.

"I think we just sold the last two seats for tonight," the clerk warned her. "I'll check."

Just her luck! Emory waited a few moments, then the clerk came back on the line. "We do have one left," he said. "First ring, center. The performance is *La Traviata,*" he added.

"Oh, wonderful!" Emory was delighted. She gave him her name and room number so that she could pick the ticket up later.

After a quick shower, Emory dressed in a beautiful emerald green satin dress with a matching jacket that she had brought along just in case her friends chose a fancy restaurant for dinner. She was pleased about getting the last ticket to the opera, and tried to make the best out of attending all alone. She'd read somewhere that it lifted your spirits to dress up, so she decided to take some extra time, putting her hair up in an elegant twist, choosing jewelry and even a bit of makeup. Who knows, Emory told herself as she appraised her reflection, I might just meet a dark, handsome, culture-loving stranger tonight.

She locked her door, realizing that she had probably met her fair quota of dark handsome strangers for the month. One, was in fact, proving to be more than she could handle.

As Emory walked across the lobby to the entertainment desk to collect her ticket, she could feel the admiring, interested glances of several men who passed her. She pretended not to notice. The young woman at the ticket desk found her ticket quickly. Emory was just signing a receipt when she heard an almost too familiar voice behind her. "Fiore. Room 2332. You're holding a ticket for me?"

"Oh— Hello," Emory said, turning around and nearly bumping into him.

"Emory?" Nick had obviously not recognized her from the back. "Gee—I didn't even see you standing there."

"Yes, I guess you didn't," Emory said smoothly, taking full advantage of the look on his face. Was it so shocking to him that she could dress up with jewelry and makeup? Men were really so silly sometimes.

He looked very nice, too, she noticed. Much more dressed up than she'd expect for a basketball game. His blue suit had been pressed and looked far more presentable than it had earlier. Or maybe she was just getting used to it? Anything was possible, Emory mused.

Under the jacket he wore a pure white shirt and a beautiful paisley silk tie. Not the funny striped one from this morning and not the zany one they'd bought in Soho. Perhaps he'd picked it up here, in one of the hotel's fancy shops. Clean shaven with his hair a bit damp from his shower, he looked too good to resist,

Emory thought. Maybe he was going out afterward, she thought, someplace special. With music and dancing. Without her. She felt hurt all over again, but tried to hide it.

"Your ticket, sir. *La Traviata,* first ring, center. The performance begins at eight," the young woman behind the desk said, checking the ticket Nick was purchasing. "If you'll just sign here," she said, pointing to a receipt.

"I thought you were going to that basketball run-off game." Now it was Emory's turn to look shocked.

"It's a *play-off,* not a run-off," Nick said, laughing at her. "I couldn't get a ticket. I decided on the opera, instead. I rarely get to go up in Boston."

"Oh, that's too bad. I usually get season tickets. You'll have to join me sometime," she said evenly, knowing already that they would probably be seeing an opera together much sooner than he suspected.

"Well, you'll have to invite me," he said with a small tight smile, as if he was sure she never would.

"How about tonight?" she said on impulse. She pulled out her ticket. "Hmm, first ring, center—" she read. "We can even share a pair of opera glasses," she observed.

"Let me see that—" He looked surprised but pleased, and took a quick glance at her ticket to compare it to his own.

"What happened to your friends—Didi and Chester?" he asked suspiciously, handing her back the ticket. Emory could tell just by the tone of his voice, he suspected that her friends were of the snooty, upper crust variety.

"Bibi and Charles," she corrected him. "They had to cancel."

"Oh, too bad," Nick said, not looking the least bit sorry. He glanced at his watch. "Shall we get a cab? It's almost seven-thirty."

"Good idea," Emory said smoothly. Walking across the lobby, she felt Nick's hand lightly on the small of her back, guiding her through the crowd. She knew outside she looked very calm about this sudden change of plans, but inside she felt as if she were sixteen again, out on her first date.

Seven

Emory couldn't recall ever enjoying an opera as much as she did with Nick. The Metropolitan Opera House at Lincoln Center was a grand and lavishly decorated theater. A marble and crystal palace, filled with beautifully dressed people, some even in tuxedoes and evening gowns. Walking in on Nick's arm, Emory felt as if she was royalty...or close to it.

Perhaps it wasn't the setting at all, but the way Nick treated her. He was the perfect escort, charming and courteous, as smooth and sophisticated tonight as he had been raucous and unconventional all day long. He was a fascinating puzzle to Emory. Just when she thought she had him all figured out, he'd surprised her again.

His taste for the opera was one surprise, and his amazingly familiarity with it, still another. He knew the score and libretto thoroughly. During the intermission he critiqued the performers with a knowledgeable air that Emory frankly found astounding.

"The soprano is not as light as I've seen in this role," he said as they sipped glasses of champagne on the second balcony of the opera house. "I think I prefer a more lyrical expression. Although her voice will be well suited to the third act," he added.

"Yes—it will," Emory said, not quite knowing what to make of this new side of him. "You never told me you knew so much about the opera."

"You never asked," he replied, a teasing light dancing in his eyes.

"Part of your police academy training?" she teased him back.

"Hardly." He laughed. "But now that you mention it, I do recall an x-rated version of some Gilbert and Sullivan tunes at our graduation review," he added.

"I can just imagine," Emory said, fascinated by the wonderful dimples that had appeared in his cheeks when he smiled. She noticed them when she first met Nick, but now they were so apparent.

"No, I *don't* think you can, Professor," he corrected her. "My parents were the opera buffs. They played it night and day. I honestly hated it as a kid... but I guess it sunk in anyway. It's one of my secret passions now," he admitted, leaning over to practically whisper the confidence.

"Oh? Why secret?" Emory asked him.

"Oh, I don't know," he said with a shrug. "Aren't secret passions more fun? Well, maybe only when you can share them with someone who has the same passion as you do," he said, answering his own question.

"Maybe," Emory said. She knew that she was staring at him, but couldn't quite pull her gaze away. His dark, warm gaze promised a passion beyond her most secret fantasies.

She was getting herself into trouble tonight. She'd known it from the first minute she'd run into him at the ticket desk. But she couldn't blame herself entirely. That she and Nick should enjoy this evening out together—and whatever might follow—really seemed fated somehow, like the romantic episodes of the opera. Then she scolded herself for being so silly. Destiny, indeed! That was true of opera's star-crossed lovers, but not in real life, she reminded herself.

The houselights flashed and it was time to return to their seats. Emory was so enthralled by the music and drama that she forgot all about her own romantic dilemma. That is, until Nick squeezed her hand during the very last scene when the heroine died in the hero's arms. Emory felt her eyes well up with tears, then thought Nick would think she was being silly. But as the houselights went up and the performers took their last bows, she noticed that he, too, had gotten a bit misty-eyed. She was shocked, but careful to hide it. So the tough guy wasn't so tough after all, she realized. The night was proving to be chock-full of revelations.

"Tissue?" she asked simply, taking one out of her purse.

"Thanks," he said, pressing it to his eyes. "Can't help it. That deathbed scene gets me every time."

"Me, too," Emory confided.

Nick suggested that they continue the evening with a late supper at a nearby French restaurant. It was one of the most fashionable cafés in the city and Emory was frankly quite surprised again at his choice. "I thought you had a craving for pastrami," she said, reminding him of their conversation that afternoon.

"Pastrami is perfect *après*-basketball," he explained, not seeming the least bit put off by her question. "But after a romantic opera set in France you have to have French food. Cassoulet, I think, and a glass of Beaujolais," he suggested.

"Oh, I see," she said. He was expanding her education at every turn.

The restaurant was decorated in a turn-of-the-century, Baroque style, with low lighting, plush, red-velvet-lined booths and a wall mural of frolicking nymphs. While enjoying the delicious food and the superb bottle of Beaujolais Nick selected, Emory was thoroughly entertained by Nick's stories of his adventures on the police force. Some tales were frightening, but some were quite funny.

One story, about chasing robbery suspects who ran down a dock and jumped in the water, had her laughing out loud. His overeager rookie partner had been driving the squad car and followed in hot pursuit, right off the dock and into the St. Charles River.

"Luckily the water wasn't that deep," Nick added. "Next car I was issued, some joker put a snorkel in the glove compartment."

"Come on, Nick. You're really teasing me now," Emory challenged him.

"Hey, this is all true," he swore. "You can't make up stuff like this. It's too weird. How about you, Professor? Don't you have any amusing adventures to relate about college life?"

"The life of a college professor might look like action and adventure from the outside," Emory teased him, "but it's hardly as glamorous as people think."

"What a shame. No fun at all?"

"We have our moments, I suppose," Emory amended. She was thinking of the thrill of seeing her articles published in a journal, or making some scholarly discovery. Hardly what Nick would call blood-curdling excitement. "Tonight is probably the most fun I've had in a long time," she admitted.

"I'm glad," he said quietly, gazing deeply into her eyes.

"The opera was just beautiful, didn't you think?" she added, her voice sounding a bit shaky, even to her own ears.

"You are just as beautiful," he said simply. "I could hardly keep my eyes on the opera."

He reached across the table and took her hand in both of his own. Emory did not pull back. His hands were warm and strong, covering hers. She didn't know what to say. Her mind was blank and she doubted she could find her voice, even if a coherent thought came to mind. He studied her hand in the candlelight, turning it over to look at her palm.

"Are you reading my fortune?"

"Maybe—" he said, glancing up at her with a devilish look in his eye. "Let's see. Very interesting," he murmured.

"Well? What's the forecast?" Emory couldn't resist encouraging him, although she didn't much believe in palm reading, or horoscopes, or any of that hocus-pocus.

"See that curvy line, there?" he said, pointing down to her hand. "And that thick line, there? Well, one is your head—intellect, reasoning. You've got plenty of that. The other is your heart—passion, desire, all that good stuff. They crisscross, right here," he said, pointing out a spot about dead center of her hand.

He suddenly looked up at her and she felt a funny lump in her throat. She swallowed hard. "So?"

"So it seems that your head has been ruling things for a while, but the heart line will soon be on top. You're in for a change, Professor," he said smugly. "A big change, I'd say."

"Nonsense," Emory said, whisking her hand back.

"Of course you'd say that now," he pointed out, laughing at her reaction. "Just wait...."

"You never mentioned that you were part Gypsy, Nick."

"Well, there are a few parts of me you still haven't been introduced to, sweetheart," he replied with a slow grin.

While Emory gave the comment some thought, Nick signaled to their waiter and asked for the check.

They found a cab quickly and were soon flying back down Broadway to their hotel. Emory noticed that Nick was uncharacteristically quiet. She told herself that he must be tired after their busy day and night out on the town. She, however, did not feel the least bit tired. She was alert and on edge, wondering what would happen next.

They collected their keys at the front desk and rode up in the elevator, side by side but not touching. Emory watched the numbers of each floor flash by and felt a knot growing larger in the pit of her stomach.

Before she could politely thank Nick for their night out, he said, "I'd better walk you to your room."

"Oh, I think I'll be all right," she said as the elevator stopped and the doors opened. "This is the Plaza."

"No, I'd feel better if I walk you," Nick insisted. "The old guard dog acting up in me again, I guess," he added, his hand resting lightly around her waist as he followed her out of the elevator.

"Okay, Rover. Suit yourself." As they approached her room, she took out her key—the modern, square plastic kind that had holes punched in it. Nick took it from her and opened her door.

"Feel better now?" she asked, turning toward him.

He looked down at her a moment, a light dancing in his dark eyes. He cupped her face in his hand, testing the silky smoothness of her cheek with his palm. "Not yet," he said, bending his head toward hers. He tasted her lips, with a soft, tantalizing motion that sent heat waves singing along Emory's limbs. She leaned her head back and moved closer, her hands stealing around his broad shoulders. He would not give in to her gentle urging, however, and continued to tease her with kisses that felt ever so slightly short of the full, passionate pressure of his mouth sealed on hers. A pressure her whole body now seemed to clamor for.

It seemed to be a game for him, she realized, the more she revealed how much she wanted him to kiss her—*really* kiss her, the way he had that first time on her doorstep—the more he drew it out, inventing new and better ways to tease her. He drew his tongue along her lower lip, followed the hollow of her cheek with his soft lips, touched her temple with sensitive kisses, explored her ear with his tongue then sucked on her earlobe. His strong tongue darting into her mouth for the briefest taste of her, then drawing away again. It was an infuriating, captivating, totally stimulating game, she realized hazily. One she'd never played before.

All rational thought was a hazy fog in her mind, all her well-intended promises to herself were now forgotten as Emory pulled Nick's head down toward hers for at least one full, satisfying kiss he seemed determined to deny her.

"Hmm—Emory, watch out. The smoke alarm out here's liable to go off any minute," he said huskily. Then he sighed, as if giving in to some urge he'd been denying, and finally pulled her up close to his hard warm body. So close she could feel his hard throbbing need through the smooth satin of her dress. Obviously he had not been immune to his own taunting tactics, she thought with some satisfaction.

"We don't have to stay out here," she suggested impulsively. "The door is open." Then she felt a knot of apprehension well up inside. What if he backed away again, as he had that first time? What would she do? It would be so awfully humiliating.

He looked down at her and for a moment she thought he was going to pull away and leave her right there in the open doorway. She didn't know what to do or say. She had never been in such a position before— wanting with all her being to coax a man into her hotel room. It was strange, like watching another person from a distance who just happened to be wearing her body. She could barely breathe, waiting for him to decide, her gaze fixed on a spot on his tie.

Then suddenly she felt him move and she moved with him, through the door that was swiftly locked behind them. The room was dark, illuminated only by the light from an open window. She heard Nick's jacket drop to the floor and he was holding her powerfully tight, his passionate strength unleashed as they stood by the bed, their lips pressed together in a deep breathtaking kiss. And then another, and another. Emory wrapped her arms around his waist as they fell onto the bed, side by side. She was intoxicated by so many sensations at once—surrounded by the feel of him, his warm, male scent, the feeling of his powerful body moving under her hands.

His hands were everywhere at once on her body. Exploring her, learning her, outlining her every peak and curve beneath the cool satin: the soft swell of her breasts, the dip of her waist, her softly rounded hips and bottom cupped in his hands. He smoothed open the buttons at the front of her dress, her lace-covered breasts suddenly bared to him. Twisting around, he bent his head to taste their hardened tips, licking and sucking through the sheer black lace. Emory closed her eyes, lost on a swelling rise of heat, her body arched toward him, the soft core of her tightening, growing hot and liquid as he kissed one breast and then the other, urging them to hard, sensitive peaks.

Every inch of her was suddenly awakened, on fire. She wanted to feel more of him, his clothes seeming an unnatural barrier that simply had to be removed. Her fingers swiftly worked loose his tie and the buttons on his shirt, one popping off and flying into space.

"Good God..." He sighed as she finally had his shirt open and pressed her cheek against his hot skin. His thick dark hair felt deliciously ticklish against her lips. With her eyes closed, she explored this new territory, finally bared to her. She sought and found one flat male nipple, and licked it to a hard peak, wanting to give him the same pleasure he'd lavished on her. She had barely touched her tongue to his skin when she felt his body writhe against her in excitement.

"My God—Emory. You are making me crazy. You're so loving and sexy. I never expected..." His voice trailed off on another sigh of satisfaction.

Barely able to stand it anymore, he pulled her up on top of him, his tongue plunging deeply into her mouth as she felt his powerful manhood press urgently up against her soft, molten center. She wanted more of him, more bare skin against bare skin, more of his slow deep kisses, more of him outside, inside, surrounding her, filling her.

This was passion, plain and simple, the kind she'd only dreamed of experiencing in some man's arms, but had never known before this night. Then Emory felt Nick pull back. Cupping her face in his hands, he gazed up at her and ran his fingers through her tumbled hair. She slipped off him and lay at his side. "You are beautiful." He sighed, staring over at her. "I never expected..." His voice trailed off.

But instead of her deepest secret passions coming true, she suddenly realized that her worst fears were about to come to pass. "But I'd better go. It's just... better."

"All right," she whispered in a confused, shaky voice. She fumbled with the front of her dress, pulling it closed. "If you want to—" She didn't want to cry in front of him, but suddenly felt as if she might.

"I—it's just better that I go now," he said.

"You already said that," she reminded him quietly as she sat up.

"I think it is," he insisted, sitting up, too. "I don't want it to be like this. Between us, I mean."

"Oh?" Emory felt stung by his words. "It's a little late in the evening for that insight, don't you think?"

"I'm sorry," he said, sighing. He ran his hands through his hair, looking as dismayed as she felt. "I want to behave... well, properly for once in my life.

Please don't make it hard for me, Emory. I'm trying to do the right thing here ... for you,'' he implored her.

"For me?" she said, standing up. "For your steady girlfriend, perhaps. But please don't try to persuade me that you're doing me any favors!"

"Steady girlfriend?" His shirt still hanging loose, he stood up and faced her. "What are you talking about? Who said anything about a girlfriend?"

"Well, isn't there one?" Emory could think of no other reason why he would seem so determined to take a gallant leave of her. "Or is it that, after a good show of seeming to be attracted to me, you just changed your mind. You don't want to mislead me and all that," she said in a rush.

"Change my mind? I think I'm *losing* my mind, if you really want to know the truth," he nearly shouted back. "One minute, I have a prim and proper professor on my hands, the next minute, you've got me about ready to explode. What's a man supposed to do?" he asked her, sounding partly confused and partly plain angry. "I don't want you thinking I'm some kind of groping teenager, all over you the minute you let down your guard long enough for a kiss ... But damn it, lady..." He sighed and shook his head. "You really are ... something."

"I am?" Emory's voice came out in a husky croak. She still thought she was going to cry, but now because Nick wasn't running away from her because he didn't find her attractive enough. It sounded as if he was finding her *too* attractive.

"Yes—" He stopped pacing around the room long enough to solemnly nod his head. "You *are*. Maybe it's you and me together. All that chemistry stuff. Whatever, it is ... something pretty hot. And you're such a class act," he added with a wave of his hand in her direction. "I just didn't want you to think I was some kind of jerk. I just wanted things to happen slower, at a more dignified pace. What you must be used to, I mean...." His voice trailed off.

He was standing with his back to her in front of the window that faced the park, his hands on his hips. Emory studied his dark silhouette, feeling as if her heart was about to burst with wanting him. She knew she had a choice, to let him leave her tonight, which was probably the right thing to do. Or to ask him to stay, which seemed to be the only thing she wanted to do.

Searching to find the words she needed to say, Emory walked over to where Nick stood and slipped her arms around his waist. Up on tiptoe, she whispered in his ear, "I don't want what I'm used to, Nick. I want you."

He turned quickly in her arms. "You really mean that?"

"I do," she whispered. "I thought before...that you just didn't want to be with me for some reason," she admitted.

"Wrong, Professor," he whispered back, burying his face in the warm curve between her neck and shoulder. "*Totally* wrong." He sighed happily as he swiftly unfastened the buttons on her dress a second time that night.

"Good...I'm glad." She sighed, losing herself to the sensations his soft lips incited as they followed his fingers, smoothing kisses over her breasts and then down farther to her rib cage and flat belly. He was kneeling in front of her, her dress fully open. He smoothed down her panty hose as his tongue edged dangerously along the waistband of her bikini underwear.

Emory gasped, her fingers sinking into his heavy shoulders for support as her legs began to tremble. He stood up, catching her nearly limp form in his arms. Kissing, they moved a few short steps to the bed and Emory realized she was quite nearly undressed, down to only her bra and underpants as she helped Nick slip out of his shirt and trousers.

He loomed above her, a dark and powerfully male figure. His body was breathtaking, a torso that could have been carved in marble by a master's hand, she mused in a distant corner of her mind. But tonight it was as if an ancient masterpiece had stepped down off a marble pedestal and into her bed, coming alive for her pleasure alone.

In that brief instant Emory longed for the feeling of Nick's full weight upon her, his body covering hers, from head to toe, the full pressure of his passion bearing down on her.

"God, you're breathtaking," he said with a sigh, his hands running the length of her body, up and back again, from the delicate silky skin at the inside of her thigh, up over her sensitive, tingling core, along her belly and breasts. Then down again, his fingers slipping beneath the edge of her panties, his fingertips seeking and finding the secret womanly core of her desire.

She tensed and shivered at his touch, but his loving words soothed her. She felt as if she were floating, unaware of anything at all but the pure, intense sensations his touch inspired. With slow delicate strokes, he brought her higher and higher, her body writhing in ecstasy at his masterful touch. She quivered and moaned his name, feeling herself go up in flames, consumed in a brilliant dance of fiery colors. She clung to his broad shoulders, her face buried in the curve of his neck, her cheek pressed against his sinewy muscle as intense waves of pleasure wracked her body in wave after wave of sensation. Just when she thought she couldn't bear another second of it, she was lifted away again, on another tide of pure and fulfilling sensation.

Finally, it was over, and she rested dazed and unmoving in his arms. "Nick—I never..." She sighed, her words trailing off breathlessly.

"Shh, just relax a minute, sweetheart," he whispered, kissing her cheek and smoothing back her hair with his hand.

But Emory didn't want to relax. She wanted to give Nick as much pleasure as he had given her. She wanted to touch him, taste him, feel him shiver with passion in her arms. Her hands smoothed down the long hard curve of his torso and hips, smoothing and massaging his muscular thighs. When she urged him with a gentle push to roll onto his back, so she could have more of him available to her, he did so willingly. "You are awake, I see," he whispered.

"Very," she managed, nodding her head over him so that her long, silky hair dragged across his chest. She covered his chest with soft kisses as her hands drifted and played over the hard shaft of his manhood. When he sighed and groaned at each soft press of her fingers, she felt an inner thrill of excitement too, almost as if he was touching her again. Her lips and tongue swirled around one flat masculine nipple, and she felt his big body tremble in her arms.

"I can't stand much more of this," he said with a sigh. "Oh, God...I wish I could, though," he murmured huskily, bringing a soft, secret smile to Emory's lips as she continued her erotic explorations.

Finally, with a groan, Nick pulled her up across his body. "God, I need you now, please—" He sighed and Emory lovingly complied. He gripped her hips and she leaned down over him. Their lips met in a deep hard kiss as he slowly moved inside her, filling her completely. They moved as one in a timeless rhythm, the deep, intense waves of pleasure overwhelming her. Nick's body moved powerfully up against hers, again and again as he held tight to her waist. From faraway, she could hear his loving, coaxing endearments as she met each movement of his body with her own. Unable to hold out any longer, Emory's body arched back, her loving core gripping him in a soul-quaking explosion. Moments later she heard him cry out her name and felt his body explode inside her in a final spasm of ecstasy.

"Emory, Emory, Emory..." he said, sighing breathlessly. She fell into his open embrace and they curled their arms around each other in an exhausted but thoroughly satisfied heap. He lifted his hand to lazily stroke her hair and she snuggled up against his warmth, feeling thoroughly loved and protected by this surprisingly wonderful man.

She couldn't quite say how this had happened. But as she drifted off to a deep, calm sleep, Emory knew that whatever the future might bring, she wouldn't have traded this night with Nick for anything.

Eight

Emory woke up the next morning in an empty bed. This did not seem odd to her at first. Then slowly, as her eyes opened and she began to sit up, she realized that she wasn't wearing a nightgown and the events of the night before came back to her in a startling rush. She and Nick had fallen asleep in each other's arms, then somewhere in the night, Nick's touch had awakened her, quickly convincing her that she wanted him all over again. She felt herself blushing at the recollection of her response to him. It was all new for her. New, and more than a little frightening.

She sat up fully, pulling the sheet up around her chest. Where was Nick? The utter stillness in the room told her that she was alone. He'd probably gone to his own room to shower and dress, she told herself. She got out of bed, intending to do the same.

But instead of feeling lighthearted and elated about her new romance, Emory felt wary and full of doubts. Last night, making love to Nick had seemed like the right thing to do, the only thing to do. But Emory was not used to so easily going with the flow, jumping headlong into the chance opportunities life offered. She had been so relieved and thrilled to realize that Nick desired her, she had let her own desire rule the moment.

But now, as the shower's cool spray beat down on her, clearing her head of last night's fuzzy afterglow, she honestly wondered if a woman like herself could ever hold the interest of a man like Nick for very long. Sure, he is fascinated with the idea of getting involved with a Harvard professor. She's a challenge for him, a novelty, a wild weekend fling in New York City that makes yet another colorful anecdote for his collection of amusing stories. She could almost hear him telling it now, how he had this case that involved a stolen painting and had to deal with this classy, Harvard babe....

Emory shut the water off and was about to pull the shower curtain back when it flew aside, seemingly under its own power. She jumped back in alarm, then realized it was Nick, holding open a huge towel for her.

"It's just me, silly," he said. He quickly wrapped the towel around her, using the gesture as an excuse to hug her close. "Hmm—you smell good," he said, his cheek pressed against her wet hair.

"Just the hotel soap," she said, slowly pulling away from him. He smelled good, too—and looked even better in a red cotton sweater and jeans. She wanted to throw her arms around him and have him carry her back to the bed. But this morning's attack of rationality overcame her once more. She walked out to the bedroom and collected her bathrobe.

"I'll be out in a minute," she said, returning to the bathroom.

"Don't take too long. I've got some hot coffee out here for you."

When she emerged again, Nick was sitting at a small table near a window that framed a view of the park. He was sipping coffee and reading the morning paper. There were some fresh croissants and strawberries at her place beside her cup.

"Great day out there," he announced cheerfully. The look in his eyes as he greeted Emory made her feel warm all over. But she simply smiled back and poured herself a cup of coffee.

"Anything wrong?" he asked her then.

"No—I'm fine," she said with a light shrug. "Really." She wished he wouldn't stare at her like that. He was too perceptive sometimes for her peace of mind. Just what she deserved for getting involved with a detective.

"You're not a morning person, I gather," he said in an understanding tone.

"No argument there," she said, smiling in spite of herself. The coffee was steaming hot. Just what she needed, Emory thought as she poured herself a large cup.

"Well, I am. It can be irritating to someone else," Nick admitted with a shrug. "I mean, if you're the slow-off-the-block type. It's really just metabolism."

"You sound as if you've run into this situation...frequently," she said, imagining all the morning tête-á-têtes he'd had with a parade of women before her.

"Enough," he admitted with a laugh. When Emory didn't laugh, too, his smile quickly faded. "Something is bothering you, Professor," he said, calmly putting his paper aside. "Out with it," he urged her.

Emory toyed with a strawberry on her plate, wondering whether to confide her morning doubts to him.

"I, uh, I was wondering when you thought we'd get back up to Boston. I do have a lot of work to finish this weekend. I haven't even marked half those papers I brought down with me. . . ." Her voice trailed off and she avoided meeting his gaze.

"So you're worried about grading papers?" Nick asked quietly.

"Yes, well. And some other things I have to catch up on." She shrugged.

"I see." Nick leaned back in his chair and crossed his arms over his broad chest. He stared at her, his lovely mouth, which she was secretly aching to kiss, was pursed in thoughtful expression. "We can leave for Boston anytime you like," he said finally. "You've certainly done more than your share of civic duty this weekend, Emory," he added in a wry tone. "I wouldn't want you to fall behind in your work."

"Oh, well. Okay." Emory shrugged and took a sip of coffee. She wished he would stop staring at her like that. It was getting very difficult for her not to just blurt out her worries. Is this how he got confessions out of suspects? The technique seemed to be working remarkably well on her.

"However," Nick added in the same slow, measured tone, "we're not going anywhere until we have a talk."

"A talk? About what?" Emory asked nervously. She strolled over to the nightstand, tightened the belt on her bathrobe and put on her glasses.

"You know about what," Nick insisted. He got up from his seat and walked toward her. "Second thoughts about last night, I guess. Right?"

"Uh—no," Emory lied. "Last night was...well, wonderful," she said sincerely.

"I thought it was wonderful, too. I want to make love to you right this very minute," he confessed. "I want to pick you up and toss you right back in that bed," he added with a wistful look at the unmade bed behind Emory. "I have ever since I came back in here," he admitted, taking another step closer.

"Nick— Just a second. Before we do anything...impulsive..." Emory stared at him over the rim of her glasses, taking another step backward. The back of her legs bumped into the bed and she nearly fell back onto it—a moment that would have given full expression to the phrase "Freudian slip" some ironically distant part of her brain observed.

"Who's about to do anything impulsive?" he contested to her surprise. "Who's about to do anything about...anything? *You're* in a hurry to get back to Boston to mark papers," he reminded her angrily. "But I have to be honest with you, I'm beginning to worry that last night was just a...well, sort of a fling for you. And now you've decided, well, it was fun, but I'm not your type, or something like that, right?"

His bluntness shocked her, but Emory suddenly realized that Nick had the courage to voice the very same fears she'd been stewing about all morning.

"I have been worried about it," Emory admitted. "But that's not what I was thinking. You make it sound like I just . . . used you."

"Well, maybe we used each other, okay? A romantic night. The opera, dinner. All that chemistry we seem to have going for us?" Nick shook his head in dismay. "That's all right. You can be honest," he said calmly. He was close to her now, looking down at her with a dark, tight expression, his arms crossed over his chest. He was an intimidating figure, Emory thought, but she willed herself to face up to him.

"If you must know the truth, I've been worried about the same thing," Emory finally admitted. "That you were using me . . . well, not really using me, but just attracted to me because we're so different. But I've been afraid this morning that it won't work. That we are too different and . . ." She'd gone this far, she thought, she might as well get it all out. "Well, I'm really afraid that you're used to women much different than me and that . . . you'll get bored."

There, she said it. She breathed out a sigh of relief. Emory had taken off her glasses and was twisting the frames in her hands as she spoke. With her final admission, she looked down at her glasses, unable to face Nick. She felt sad.

"You know, you look so smart and logical and sane," Nick said softly. "Nobody would ever guess what a wacky dame you really are, Professor," he said with a soft laugh as his big hands gripped her shoulders.

"Wacky? Why am I wacky?" Emory asked him.

"Who's getting bored with you? I'm crazy about you," he admitted in a low, solemn whisper. "I haven't felt this way about a woman since high school—Mary

Ellen Gallagher, head cheerleader at St. Michaels, who wouldn't even glance twice in my direction," he explained. "See, I was worried about the same thing. That my being a cop would be fun for you at first, but it would embarrass you after a while. It's happened to me before," he admitted, "so I wouldn't want it to happen again."

Emory heard the pain in his voice and wondered about the woman who had hurt him. She never wanted to be remembered by him that way, not in a million years. But she also knew she had to be honest.

"Nick, I'm crazy about you, too," she admitted. "Everything is so new with you, so much fun. I feel like a different person. I don't even know myself sometimes," she said, thinking mostly about how she'd responded to him last night in bed. She felt her cheeks get warm with that recollection. It was so hard to put into words how she felt. Emory hoped Nick would understand her nervous, emotional rambling. "I want to see what will happen . . . but I'm scared. We are so different. What if it doesn't work?"

"I'm scared, too," he admitted with a long sigh. He stared into her eyes, and she slipped her arms around his waist. He pressed his cheek against her hair and kissed her. "But I think I'm more afraid not to try. Do you know what I mean?"

Emory nodded. She didn't know what to say. When he held her like this, she could barely think.

"Maybe I should go," Nick whispered. "So that you can pack up and think things over a little."

"Don't go," Emory whispered back. "Not yet." She was scared witless about embarking upon a real relationship with Nick, but she knew now she couldn't turn her back on something this good, something this powerful.

"What about getting back home to mark those papers?" Nick laughed softly as his arms embraced her slender form. "I wouldn't want to distract you from your work, Professor."

"You already have," Emory admitted as his lips moved from her hair to her cheek and then down to the soft corner of her mouth. "I think it's too late to worry about that now. Besides, the shuttle runs all day, every half hour."

"I'm in no rush," Nick murmured right before their lips met in a deep, soul-wrenching kiss.

"Neither am I," Emory said with a sigh as she felt the belt on her bathrobe unknot and slip to the floor. Just as Nick had promised, he suddenly lifted her off her feet and tossed her onto the unmade bed.

"Nick!" Emory's squeal of surprise was quickly muffled by another kiss when he swooped down beside her.

This love affair was a long shot, to be sure. They could both admit it. But she knew she'd never forgive herself for not taking the gamble, for once in her life, taking the less sensible course of action. When Nick held her close like this, her doubts disappeared. She felt as if nothing could ever go wrong for them.

After making love, Nick held Emory close. She knew now that the night before hadn't been merely a romantic fluke. Their lovemaking had been just as intense and remarkable today, if not more so. Her heart felt full to overflowing with feelings for this man, yet she didn't have the courage to put any of them into words. It was too soon, she decided. Much too soon.

"You're not going to believe this," Nick said finally. He stretched out beside her with his hands folded behind his head.

"Try me." Propped on her elbow, Emory took secret pleasure in simply looking at him. He was absolutely gorgeous.

"All that...activity made me hungry," he admitted.

"Again?" Emory laughed. The man had a big appetite in all categories, that was for sure. "We just had breakfast."

"A few berries and a roll? I don't call that breakfast," Nick argued. "The relevant question at this point, Professor, is do we order room service or drag ourselves out of bed and down to a restaurant?"

But before she could decide, there was a knock on the door. She got up to answer it. "Bellman," a voice called out from behind the door. "A delivery for you."

"Just a minute." Emory jumped up and looked around for her bathrobe. "Maybe room service is telepathic and they're sending up a pizza," she quipped to Nick as she tightened the belt on her robe.

"I wish. One with mushrooms and pepperoni," he added wistfully.

Emory swung the door open and received the package. It was not a pizza. Wrapped in paper, it was a large arrangement of flowers. "Thank you," she said, handing the bellman a tip.

"Nick, you really shouldn't have." Setting the flowers down, Emory began tearing off the small white envelope that was taped to the outside of the wrapping paper.

"I'm glad you feel that way about it—" He got out of bed and wrapped a towel around his hips. "Because I didn't."

Emory was embarrassed for assuming the flowers were from Nick. But who else could have sent them? She quickly pulled out the card and read it.

It was a pleasure meeting you and your associate yesterday. I am attending the arts festival in Venice and will return to New York in a few weeks. I look forward to speaking to you again about the Newland collection—and more about "private" passions?

Best, Nolan

"It's from Babcock," Emory announced to Nick, who was now standing beside her.

"Let me see," he said, taking the card. He read it quickly. "What does he mean by this 'private passions' line?" he said, sounding a bit jealous, she thought.

"You know, what he said about collectors purchasing stolen works for their own enjoyment?" Emory reminded him.

"Oh . . . right." Nick nodded, watching her tear off the paper.

"Wow!" Nick gave a slow, low whistle. "The guy believes in saying it with flowers, doesn't he?"

They both stared down in shock at Babcock's floral selection—a bouquet of brilliant yellow tulips in a dark blue glazed pottery vase.

"This couldn't be a coincidence...could it?" Emory asked, glancing up at Nick.

"Not very likely. This is what I'd call a special order," Nick said with a laugh.

"Yes—" Emory said, feeling goose bumps on her skin. "I guess it was."

Nick was gleeful, hardly noticing Emory's dismay as the reality of the situation began to sink in. She had never dealt so closely with a criminal before. Now it seemed that one was sending her flowers, with little innuendo-laden notes attached.

"This is terrific!" He turned to her and gripped her by the shoulders. "We've got this guy just where we want him. All because of *you,* sweetheart." Nick kissed her quickly on the lips and then pulled her close for a quick, hard hug.

"Well, you helped a *little,*" she added generously.

"A little," he admitted with a grin.

Emory and Nick were back in Boston by the early afternoon. Between his threats of fainting from hunger, Nick had managed to pick up his car at the airport parking lot and drive them directly to a seaport café. It was a beautiful afternoon and Emory felt wonderful. The whole world and everyone in it looked perfect to her. She totally forgot about the papers she had to grade, or preparing lecture notes for tomorrow's classes. What was it about Nick that made her feel this way? she wondered, glancing at his handsome profile as he drove them back to her apartment.

They carried Emory's luggage upstairs and she prepared to make some coffee. Although Nick had suggested that he leave after the coffee so that she could do some work, his good intentions didn't last very long. Together, in Emory's small kitchen, they gathered cups, cream and sugar. Emory felt Nick's arms circle her waist from behind and his warm lips search out the smooth skin at the back of her neck. It was only a few moments later that the decanter of coffee was left standing to cool on the countertop while Emory led Nick to her bedroom.

Later, they held each other close in Emory's antique four-poster as the last rays of daylight filtered through the half-drawn curtains.

"You're awfully quiet again, Professor," Nick observed. "Not another bout of second thoughts I hope?"

"No, not at all." Emory shook her head and smoothed her hand over the soft dark hairs on his chest. "Just the opposite."

"Good news for our side," he replied. "I think I'm beginning to read you pretty well. I'll admit, it's still a challenge at times."

"I should hope so." Emory laughed. "I wouldn't want to be too obvious and bore you."

"Obvious?" Nick laughed. "Mysterious is more like it."

"Me? Mysterious?" For some reason the charge made Emory self-conscious. She sat up to get a better look at him. "What's so mysterious about me?"

"You never talk about yourself, for one thing. There's a lot I don't know about you," he admitted, settling against the pillows.

"Well, we haven't known each other all that long," she replied, avoiding his gaze. "And, I guess it's hard for me to talk about myself." Maybe Nick was right, she thought. She had always been a very private person and it was hard to let anyone get really close. Perhaps it was time to let down her defenses. Perhaps Nick was the first man she could really trust.

"Sure, I understand," he said, and she believed him. "There's no rush. It's just that I'm curious about you." He smiled at her warmly, his dark eyes glowing. "What you looked like when you were a little girl, for instance. Any brothers or sisters? That sort of thing."

"Well, let's see," Emory said thoughtfully. "I have one older sister, Paige. She lives in London right now. Her husband is a big corporate type. International law, or something. We were never really that close," she admitted. "But I do adore their children, David and Jane. They come to stay with me twice a year. They're really adorable."

"Hmm, very good," Nick said encouragingly. She knew he sensed how hard it was for her to talk like this, but it also felt good to share these thoughts with Nick. She really did want him to know her.

Responding to Nick's gentle questions, Emory told him a bit more about upbringing and family. He already had some idea about the way she was raised in a Back Bay mansion—the private boarding schools, the lessons, the dignitaries and celebrities her parents entertained at lavish parties, or at their summer home on Martha's Vineyard.

What he couldn't guess, though, and what she only hinted at, was the loneliness she'd felt growing up in the vast, cheerless household with only her older sister Paige or the servants for company. She'd retreated to the companionship of books and so she'd become the family "egghead" while her sister played the role of the beautiful society "deb."

"But what about what you looked like when you were a little girl? You skipped that one, Emory," he pointed out.

"Oh, well...let's see. When I was a little girl I looked sort of...shorter," she replied with a teasing grin. "I was a real bookworm, too."

"What a surprise," Nick said blandly. "What about later, in high school, when did you get so pretty?"

Emory squirmed. She didn't consider herself all that attractive, although Nick's flattery was certainly a great boost to her ego. "Oh, I don't know," she said breezily. "What about you? Why do I get all the questions and you haven't answered any yet?"

"I knew that was coming." Nick laughed out loud and sat up straighter against the pillows. "Okay, shoot. What do you want to know?"

"Oh, I don't know." Emory shrugged, not sure where to start. The truth was she wanted to know everything. Especially about Nick's past relationships with other women. "Let's just skip it for now."

"No." Nick shook his head emphatically. "Something is on your mind, Emory. I can tell. What did you want to ask me about?" he demanded.

It was hard for Emory to be so direct, but she took a deep breath and plunged right in. Something Nick had said during their talk that morning had been needling her all day.

"Well, this morning, when we had our talk," Emory began hesitantly, "you mentioned something about a relationship that didn't work out... I was wondering about that," she admitted.

She was really wondering about it because Nick had made a comparison of that situation to their new romance. But she didn't want to admit that to him. Not just yet.

"Oh, right." Nick nodded. "Well, there's not too much to say." He looked uncomfortable and Emory wondered if she should have pushed him. "Her name was Audrey. She's an attorney and we met on a case." Just as Nick had met me, Emory thought. "We got along pretty well at first," he explained. "Well, better than pretty well, I guess. We began to live together and we were talking about getting married... Well, I guess I was doing most of the talking," Nick added, looking out at the harbor.

"You don't have to say any more if you don't want," Emory said quietly. "Let's talk about something else, okay?"

"I'm okay. I can tell you about it." Nick suddenly turned and looked directly at her. "Things just went sour on us. I think now that there wasn't all that much there to begin with. Audrey liked the novelty of living with a cop for a while, but then the fun wore off," Nick said harshly.

He went on to explain that she became impossible to please. He could see that she was suddenly embarrassed to socialize with him among her colleagues and friends. It hurt him to admit it, but it was true.

"I thought we could work through that if she had really wanted to. Then I found out she was cheating on me. Some investment banker," Nick said ruefully. "She didn't even try to deny it. She moved out that night and has since married the guy and moved to New York. I guess the whole episode had made me a bit wary of getting involved with the smart, classy type," he admitted.

"I can understand that," Emory said quietly. She didn't want Nick to know it, but the story had given her chills. The sweet cloud she'd been floating on all day was suddenly sent crashing down to earth. Nick didn't seem to see it, but Emory secretly thought their match was more like this past romance than he realized. Was he trying to relive the past in some way? To correct an old mistake by pairing up with her? Emory certainly hoped not. Besides, she told herself, it was a little early in the relationship for such conclusions.

"Emory—" As if reading her mind, Nick reached toward her and took her hand again. "I know what I said this morning sounded like I was making a comparison to the past, but that's not the way I see it at all," he assured her. "You and Audrey are as different as night and day. It's not that same thing between us at all," he promised.

"I hope not," Emory said sincerely. "It's just that you did say we're the same type," she reminded him, her voice hanging on a tremulous note.

"I meant to say, I was always gun-shy of involvements with a certain type of woman...until I met you. You're different, and everything between us is different for me. I really mean it."

"I know you do," Emory said, putting her arms around him. She knew Nick was sincere, and hoped that it was really true. She felt suddenly protective of him and angry at any woman who could have treated him so heartlessly.

As she held Nick close, Emory knew she had more to tell Nick about herself. A lot more, actually. She also had a failed relationship in her past, but for some reason she was unable to share this information just yet. Even though he had spared nothing with you, Emory reminded herself. She felt guilty, but couldn't help it. Another time, perhaps. They'd have plenty of close talks like this in the days to come, she hoped.

Nick would probably be surprised to hear that she'd once been married. But it was hard to talk about it to him just now. She wondered if he would understand, or would he simply deduce that something was weird about her for marrying a man twenty years her senior when she was still a graduate student. And Nick seemed so sensitive about not being part of her academic circle, she didn't want him to feel intimidated when she described Winston.

Professor Winston Cahill had been her academic idol and mentor for many years before the slightest hint of romance had entered their relationship. Intellectually they'd been a perfect match and Emory was extremely grateful to him for all the attention and encouragement he'd given her over the years. She was uncomfortable with men her own age, although many were attracted to her. She got so nervous on dates, she could hardly hold a normal conversation. But with Winnie, she didn't worry about her clothes, or makeup, or any of those things. Perhaps that was why when their relationship grew more romantic, she didn't pull back. She felt safe with Winnie and she was flattered that a man universally acknowledged as a brilliant scholar could even find her remotely interesting.

But in two short years Emory began to face the hard truth that a marriage needed more than intellectual compatibility and mutual respect in order to thrive and grow. Winston realized it, too. Their parting was difficult and bittersweet, but Winston made it as easy for her as possible. Although she didn't see him much since he'd retired to Italy, he remained her devoted friend, adviser and admirer.

Now in Nick's arms, Emory thought she had finally found the kind of deep, overwhelming passion she'd only dreamed about, the kind of passion she glimpsed from a distance, in masterpieces or symphonies. Nick

gave her all that—and more. It was quite unbeliev-
able, but true. She couldn't tell him that yet, though,
she decided. It was much too soon. The feelings, too
new.

"So while we're on the subject of old lovers," Nick
asked pointedly, as if reading her mind, "what about
this Leo character you mentioned last week? How does
he fit into the picture?"

Emory laughed softly. "Oh, I don't think our relationship will change my arrangement with Leo very
much," she replied lightly. As if on cue, the fluffy orange cat walked up to the bed and nuzzled Emory's
hand, hoping to be petted.

"It won't, huh?" Nick said, sitting up. He rubbed
the back of his neck. "Well, maybe I don't like that
idea," he admitted gruffly.

"Nick, don't be so silly. I think you and Leo will get
along fine. In fact, he'd probably love to join us right
now," Emory said mischievously.

"Now? Here?" She nodded. "In bed, you mean?"
Nick sat bolt upright, looking totally shocked at her
brazen suggestion. "In *this* bed?"

"Why not?" Emory asked innocently. She looked
down at Leo and patted the blanket. The cat instantly
sprang up onto the blanket beside her. "Nick meet
Leo—short for Leonardo da Vinci."

The cat delicately stepped across Emory's body to
investigate Nick. "This is Leo? I thought—" One dark
eyebrow cocked, he fixed her with an accusing expression. "You purposely tricked me into thinking that Leo
was a man."

"I never said Leo was a man. That was your as-
sumption," Emory reminded him.

"One you purposely encouraged. Why?" he persisted.

"Well—" Emory petted the cat, who had settled down purring in the comfortable, quilted valley between her body and Nick's. "I guess I thought if you thought I had a man in my life, it would scare you off," she admitted.

"But you didn't count on the fact that I don't scare off that easily," Nick pointed out.

"Lucky for me you don't," Emory said in a low, sweet voice. She smiled softly up at Nick and he swiftly leaned over to capture her mouth with a long, deep kiss.

"Lucky for both of us," Nick murmured, moving closer. The cat, caught between them, wriggled free and leapt off the bed with an insulted meow.

"We'll catch up later, buddy," Nick called after him as he pulled Emory close.

Nine

"**M**ore linguine?" Nick held out the bowl of his delicious pasta primavera, but Emory put her hands over her plate.

"No way, I'm stuffed. I couldn't eat another bite." She sighed and smiled at him. "It was delicious ... as usual."

"Thank you." He dipped his head in a mock bow. "I love to cook for an appreciative audience."

"If I get any more appreciative of your cooking, I'm going to need a new wardrobe," Emory complained, feeling the tightness of the waistband of her skirt.

Nick was indeed an excellent cook, treating her to his complete repertoire over the past two weeks, which included not only Italian recipes, but Cajun, French, Oriental and good old-fashioned Yankee specialties. The man was a kitchen magician, it seemed to Emory. He could take any combination of ingredients, and come up with a perfect, gourmet entrée sooner than she could say microwave pot pie.

After spending their first weekend together, they'd quickly fallen into a routine of seeing each other nearly every night. Emory would come to Nick's house—a great apartment in a renovated warehouse on the waterfront. Tantalizing smells would assault her senses from the moment she entered. He never seemed to tire of cooking up delicious surprises.

Emory was a disaster in the kitchen and when Nick came over they often sent out, or tried many of the small, interesting cafés in her neighborhood. And spent a great deal of time in bed, Emory realized. Well, in bed, in the shower, on the Persian rug, the antique love seat, Nick's leather stratolounger...

Emory blushed to review the many and various places their lovemaking had led them in the last weeks. She worried sometimes that their feelings for each other were so intense, so incendiary. Didn't flash fires burn out quickly? But it was too late to worry, or even try to control the wondrous passion she experienced in Nick's arms.

It was true that recovering the painting had brought them together and as the case developed, Emory sometimes wondered what would happen when the case was resolved. Would they run out of things to talk about? They did seem to talk about it often—the next steps to take when Babcock returned from Europe, the latest news Nick collected from various sources. Nick knew the exact flight the art dealer had taken to leave the country and when he was booked to return. Checking up on the list of phone records from Emory's home and office, Nick often asked Emory about various connections he thought were worth investigating in regard to Babcock's accomplices.

It was exciting to be part of the investigation, like stepping into a mystery novel, Emory thought at times, one where she was allowed to fall in love with the handsome investigator.

But the painting wasn't the only thing they talked about, she'd remind herself. They had also had many more close talks about themselves, like that first night in her apartment. Emory had finally told Nick about her marriage. He had seemed a bit annoyed at first that she had waited so long to tell him something so important about herself. But he soon cooled down and tried to understand her reasons for holding back. Emory thought he also understood why she had made the choice she did when she was younger, and that was important to her.

Emory had to admit that when she first met Nick, she had many preconceived notions about him and some of them, not very positive. But as she learned more about him, she came to feel foolish for her limited views. She was secretly ashamed of herself. Nick was a revelation. He was, in fact, an extraordinary man who she deeply respected for reasons too numerous to list. His cooking being only one of them.

"I like my girls with a little meat on their bones," he said leaning over and playfully squeezing her thigh under the table.

"So, all this cooking is a secret plot to fatten me up, huh?"

"But I like you just the way you are, Professor," Nick replied with one of his dazzling smiles. His fingertip followed the curve of her cheek, wandering down her neck to the V-shaped neckline of her sweater.

"I wouldn't change a single freckle on your gorgeous—" his finger dipped into the lacy edge of her bra, her nipple instantly hardening "—person."

"Nick—stop," Emory said weakly as his lips drew closer to her own. "I want to clean up the kitchen for you—so you won't have to do it tomorrow—morning—" Emory's voice trailed weakly away as Nick's lips hungrily roamed her neck and his fingers moved lightly over her breasts.

"The dishes can wait," Nick murmured huskily, his beard-roughened cheek rubbing pleasantly against her soft skin. "But I don't think I can."

"But I want to— Oh!" was all she could manage before Emory was adding the colorful area rug under Nick's kitchen table to their list.

After making love, they cleaned up the kitchen together, dressed in bathrobes. "Nick, I was thinking," Emory began in a hesitant voice as she dried a frying pan. "Why don't we go out this weekend? To a play or a movie?"

"Sure, I love the movies." Nick stored some leftovers in his vast overstocked freezer.

"There's a terrific new French film at the Metro."

"Oh, really?" he replied, not sounding very enthused. "How about that new action movie, just around the corner over here?"

"You mean *Tough Cops III?*" Emory asked dismally.

"Yeah, that's it. Have you seen the first two?"

"Uh, no. I must have missed them. Did you?"

"Terrific movies. I've seen them a few times each," Nick enthused. "I'll pick them up for you at the video store."

"Great," Emory said weakly, grabbing another pot to dry. "Maybe we can compromise. See the tough cops movie one night and the French film another?" she suggested.

"Oh, sure, honey," Nick said sweetly. "That's a good idea."

Emory finally smiled. She was worried for a moment that this was going to be their first disagreement. But see how easily things worked out when two mature, rational adults just tried to compromise, she silently soothed herself.

They went into the living room and Nick flicked on the TV, automatically turning to a show he wanted to watch. It was a rerun sixties comedy with a police theme on a cable channel, one of Nick's favorites.

"Hey, this is the episode where Tooty gets kidnapped," he said excitedly. "I love this one."

"I don't think I've ever seen it," Emory said honestly. Not that she considered it a serious lapse in her education. She didn't have the heart to tell Nick she really wanted to watch a special about archaeological research in India that was on the public broadcasting channel. She took some work out of her briefcase and sat beside Nick marking papers while he thoroughly enjoyed the sitcom "classic."

The next two weeks brought more such situations, where a clash in tastes and interests was strikingly apparent to Emory. She was not always as compliant as she had been that first night, however. Compromising by seeing two movies in one weekend, or putting on two television sets in different rooms was not always the answer, either, she realized.

The other person could always tell that their partner wasn't really having a good time at the obscure French film, or the Boston Red Sox double-header, or watching reruns from the golden age of television or a documentary about van Gogh. It was as if Nick was squirming, yawning and fidgeting his way through some event for her sake. Well, how the heck was she supposed to enjoy herself?

This compromising technique was encouraged by so many articles in women's magazines about relationships she'd read over the years. So, of course, when she finally had a relationship with a man, Emory assumed it would work. But it didn't really work out that well in practical application, Emory decided. Not for her, at least.

What was the solution, then? She honestly didn't know. She only hoped that as time went on, she would figure out some better method. She had to, Emory realized. At first she'd had complete intellectual compatibility without passion. Now she had all the passion a woman could wish for—and a quirky synchronization in personalities with Nick—that was for sure. But in other ways they were as opposite as two people could be and as their differences became more evident, Emory worried about their future.

Oh, she adored Nick completely. There was no question about that. He'd made her so happy in the last few weeks she was practically walking on air. Everyone who knew her remarked upon the changes they saw so clearly. The color in her cheeks, the way she wore her hair, or even walked into a room. She was a woman in love, no doubt about it. It was common knowledge among her friends—although she had somehow neglected to tell Nick. It was so hard for her to say the words out loud. They hardly knew each other two months, she reminded herself. But sometimes, it felt as if she'd known him forever.

Whenever Emory became dismayed at their clashes of incompatibility, she soon recalled the plus side of their partnership. So far, that had been enough to keep her temper on a low simmer and her spirits optimistic. Well, most of the time.

The night Nick announced that they were invited to a softball picnic on the upcoming weekend, Emory felt a tight knot twist in the pit of her stomach.

"You'll have a great time," Nick promised. "We do it every year, as soon as the weather gets nice. It's a whole gang of guys from the department, their wives, girlfriends, kids...mothers-in-law. We stake out a whole bunch of tables at Memorial Park and play softball, barbecue, drink our fair share of beer. You'll have a great time," he promised her.

"Sounds like a lot of fun." Emory nodded and smiled, pushing her glasses a bit higher on her nose.

"Oh, it is. We sometimes have over a hundred people there. It's a good thing we're mostly cops. If not, we'd probably get a summons for outrageous partying in a public area."

"Probably." Emory smiled vaguely, then looked back down at the book she was reading. The picnic sounded positively dreadful to her. She hated gatherings like that—crowded, noisy, confused, and uncomfortable. She couldn't play softball if her life depended on it and barbecued food gave her an upset stomach. She wondered if she could pretend to have the flu when the big day arrived. Would Nick mind so awfully if she didn't go with him?

Then Emory reminded herself that part of her strong attraction to Nick was the way he persuaded her to do things she wasn't accustomed to doing. This softball picnic definitely fell into that category. Across the room, he was already dragging out bats, balls and monstrous-looking fielding gloves from the back of his closet. Despite herself, Emory found the serious expression on his face most endearing.

"Here, sweetheart," he said, handing her a softball glove. "Try this one on for size."

Emory thought the glove was big, smelly and weighed about a ton and a half. She was about as likely to catch a softball in it as she was to catch one between her teeth. But to please Nick, she did as she was told.

"This way?" she asked, putting down her book.

"Great . . . you nearly put it on the right hand, too," he encouraged her. After adjusting her glove, he took a few steps back across the room, then tossed a softball at her. "Here, catch!"

"Nick! What are you doing?" Emory held the glove up in front of herself as if it was a protective shield. "I can't catch that—"

The ball ricocheted off the tip of her glove and hit her squarely in the forehead. "Ouch!" She instinctively raised her hand to touch her head and succeeded in knocking off her glasses with the unwieldy mitt.

"Honey? Are you okay?" Nick was instantly kneeling at her side, trying to assess the damage. "Gosh, I'm sorry. Let me see. Maybe you need some ice," he soothed her, trying to get a good look at her forehead.

"Didn't I ever tell you that I once failed phys ed?" Emory asked as she rubbed her aching forehead. "I'm really an accident waiting to happen anywhere there are bats and balls."

"Honey, it was my fault. I shouldn't have surprised you like that," Nick said, leading her into the kitchen.

He wrapped some ice in a cloth and pressed it to the swelling mound on her brow.

"That's not it at all. I'm just not cut out for sports. I think you'd better know this right now, Nick. I'll only embarrass both of us at that picnic next week, believe me."

The bump on her forehead didn't really hurt very much, but Emory looked up at Nick from below her ice pack with the most mournful expression she could muster. She hoped he would have some mercy on her and say it was all right if she skipped the picnic.

"Don't worry, sweetheart," he said, stroking the back of her hair. "I don't want you to get all bent out of shape about a dumb picnic. We'll just practice some hitting and fielding. You'll do fine."

"Oh, dear." Emory slumped in her chair with a groan.

"Does it hurt that bad, honey? Maybe you should take some aspirin," Nick said, searching a kitchen cupboard.

The morning of the picnic, Nick was in such high spirits he hardly noticed that Emory was unusually quiet. After thinking over her choices, she decided pretending to be sick was too dishonest. She could grit her teeth, just this once, and try to enjoy herself, Emory decided. If she absolutely hated it, she could find some excuse to persuade Nick to take her home.

With the Jeep loaded up with picnic food and sports equipment, they set out early for the big party. Nick's gang of friends greeted him like a long lost brother, slapping his back and pumping his hand. Nick introduced Emory proudly and his friends were quite welcoming. But everybody seemed to know each other so well and talked over so many old stories and mutual friends that Emory felt quite out of place.

Emory felt so awkward attempting to fit into the conversations that she was actually relieved the group split up and headed for the softball fields. She followed Nick dutifully, feeling her nervousness grow. The bump on her forehead had barely healed. She secretly feared what was in store for her, out here in the wide open spaces.

She was given a position in the far reaches of left field and batted last. When she took her position on the field, she was so far away she could hardly hear what anybody was saying. This was perfect, she told herself. Nobody will hit the ball way out here in a million years.

And nobody did, much to her relief. That is, until the fifth inning when her team was ahead by three runs and the other team had bases loaded. A big burly guy, who everyone called Stomper, came up to the plate. So far, he'd swung out five times. But this time, he whacked one into the ozone.

"Get under it! Get under it!" Emory could hear Nick yelling at her from his spot at third base.

Running at full speed, Emory tried to follow the ball in the sky, as Nick had taught her. Keep your eye on the ball, he'd drummed into her. She ran and ran. Her lungs were burning. The ball came closer and closer. She was almost in line with it, reaching out as it dropped, stretching to get her glove out far enough. Everyone on the field seemed to be yelling a million different directions at her. Finally, there it was, dropping into her glove as she stretched. If she could only hold onto it now, that would be a miracle! Her feet flew out from under her on the slippery grass and before she had a second to look up, she was toppling into a huge metal tub filled with ice water, beer and soda cans.

Emory was so shocked that at first all she could do was sit there, sopping wet, in the middle of the tub, cans bobbing all around her. The ice water made her muscles instantly stiff and it felt almost impossible to move. She felt so mortified, she thought she was going to cry.

It was only seconds until people ran over to rescue her, but it seemed like hours. Everyone was looking at her, trying not to laugh, but it really was impossible not to. Even Nick was laughing a little as he pulled her up out of the water. "Honey, are you okay? Good thing you landed sitting down," he added. "You could have gotten hurt."

"Good thing." Emory felt her chin trembling as she stood on shaky legs, her waterlogged shorts clinging to her legs and drooping down so that she had to clutch at her belt to keep from losing them altogether.

"Oh, honey, come on now. It was an accident," Nick soothed her, putting his arm around her. The players were taking their positions on the field again and he led her to a quiet spot on the sidelines, under the trees. "You caught the ball," he praised her.

"I did?" Emory asked, looking down at her empty glove.

"Well...almost," he corrected himself. "But it was a fine effort. You really gave it your all."

"Unfortunately, my *all* could only land me in the soda tub. Hardly the Hall of Fame," she sniffed, now almost crying.

"What are you crying about? We're all friends here. Heck, that was the high point of the game. Folks are

going to be telling that story for a long time,'' Nick said
jovially.

His comment made Emory start crying in earnest.
"They are all friends," she sniffed. "Your friends, not
mine. I feel like such a moron. Can't we please go
home?"

"Honey, you're just upset." Nick tried to hug her,
but she held herself like a board in his arms. Finally, he
gave up and pulled back. "We can't go home. We just
got here. We didn't even have anything to eat yet."

"I'm not hungry," Emory sniffed. "I'm all wet."

"There's a pair of shorts in the back of the Jeep.
Why don't you change and then maybe you'll feel better. Okay?" Nick coaxed her.

Emory sighed. She knew when she was beat. Not
even a near drowning in a tub of ice water was going to
persuade Nick to go home early.

"Okay," she said. She pulled off her mitt and
handed it to him. "See you later."

"Be careful now," Nick warned her fondly as he
trotted off to join the game again.

Emory changed from her shorts into a pair of Nick's
that were baggy, gray sweatshirt material. She looked
so awful, she wanted to crawl into a hole. She tried ty-
ing her sweater around her waist, but that looked even
worse.

For the next few hours, she sat with a group of
women who had declined to play and claimed she was
brave to have even attempted the softball field. They
were busy barbecuing hamburgers and hot dogs, chasing after the children and gossiping. Mostly about each
other, Emory discovered.

She wondered what they said about her each time she
got up to walk around. Probably agreed that she and

Nick were the original odd couple and speculated on how long the romance would last. They were all very nice to her, but she couldn't help feeling as if she had crashed a meeting of a private club.

It was nearly dusk when Nick was finally ready to leave. Emory sat beside him in the Jeep's front seat in stony silence. The barbecued food she'd eaten churned ominously in her stomach. She might have known. It never agreed with her.

"You okay?" Nick finally asked.

"My stomach hurts," Emory admitted.

"Maybe you ate too much," Nick said.

"Well, I didn't have much else to do there, did I? Not after my little collision with the ice tub."

"You could have talked to people more," Nick pointed out. "You didn't have to just sit there... well, like you were waiting for a bus or something."

"I talked to people. I talked to everyone," Emory defended herself. "I just ran out of things to talk about. I mean, how much can a person discuss the relative superiority of potato chips with ridges, or those without?"

"It couldn't have been that boring for you," Nick grumbled.

"After the chip question, we progressed onto dips—the bottled kind versus the kind in the envelope that you add to sour cream."

"I guess you didn't have such a good time after all," Nick said evenly, although she could tell by the tight set of his shoulders he was angry with her.

"I guess I have had worse afternoons," Emory replied, trying unsuccessfully to make light of it.

"Where, at the dentist?"

"Perhaps," she agreed tartly. She crossed her arms over her chest.

"Well, I had a good time. I'm sorry you didn't enjoy my friends, though."

"That's not what I meant at all," Emory said, feeling he was being terribly unfair.

Nick didn't reply. He looked straight ahead as he drove and Emory felt very upset. She hated arguing with him, but she hated the silent treatment even more. She also hated the way she'd sounded, complaining like a shrew, like a snob, like a spoiled brat. But she couldn't seem to stop herself. It was all his fault, anyway, she silently stewed. Hadn't she warned him that the event would be a disaster for her?

Ten

They communicated in monosyllables over the phone for the next few days. Nick had suddenly decided to help a friend out by taking over his night shift that week, so there was little opportunity to see each other. He was purposely avoiding her, Emory thought sadly. She sat at her office desk staring into space, too distracted with thoughts of Nick to work.

Being such a novice at relationships with men, Emory had to tackle the crisis the only way she knew how—library research. She'd had plenty of time the last few nights alone to read up on their problems in some self-help relationship books she'd found in the library. As the books and magazine articles suggested, she thought about a special evening alone at her apartment to smooth things over between them. Candlelight, flowers, a jazz piano CD he had recently introduced her to playing softly in the background. They could have an honest talk and clear the air.

She would even try to serve Nick a nice dinner for once. Not cook it herself, of course. That wouldn't be relaxing for either of them. But there were plenty of gourmet shops in town. He would appreciate the effort, she was sure.

Emory mulled over her tactics and stared down that phone, still afraid to make the first diplomatic overture. As if on cue, the phone rang and it was Nick.

"I have some news for you about the case," he said in that same abrupt tone he'd been using lately. "Babcock's booked on a return flight to New York from Stockholm on Friday. We can probably expect a call any day next week."

"Oh, great," Emory replied. She felt a fluttery knot in her stomach, but knew it had little to do with the news about Babcock.

"Well, that's it," Nick said. "You know what to do by now when he calls, I'm sure."

"Of course," Emory said. They'd only gone over it about a million times. She sensed that Nick was about to hang up and forced herself to keep the conversation going. "I'm glad you called. I wanted to ask you something," Emory continued with forced brightness.

"What's up? I'm pretty busy here."

"Well, I wondered if you were working late on Friday night," Emory began nervously. He wasn't going to make it easy for her, was he? "Would you like to come over for dinner?"

"Dinner? At your house?" He might have been mad at her, but the possibility of her actually cooking something for him was far too fascinating to resist.

"Yes—dinner. You know, that meal you eat a few hours after lunch?" she asked tartly.

"Wait a second, let me check my calendar." My, my, Emory thought, wasn't he suddenly the formal one? Was he already making dates with other women? Then she realized he had to check his unusual work schedule. "Does this dinner invitation mean that your party was cancelled?" Nick asked, coming back on the line.

"What party?"

"I have a note, right on that night, that you and I are going to some sort of faculty party," Nick reported.

Emory quickly fumbled through some piles of paper on her desk and found her calendar. "Oh...you're right. I nearly forgot. I really have to go to that," she said with a sigh. "You don't have to come if you don't want to," she said on impulse, sensitive to his pun.

"Oh, you've changed your mind? You don't want me to come?" he replied.

"No—not at all. Of course I want you to come." Now what had she gone and done? He'd taken her comment completely the wrong way. "I just don't want you to feel you *have* to come, that's all."

"The way I forced you to go to the picnic, you mean?"

The unmentionable cat had been sprung from its week-old bag. Emory was actually relieved.

"You didn't force me to go to that. I wanted to go... sort of," she said lamely. "It's just that I can understand if you don't want to go with me on Friday night. I can go by myself and have you here for dinner on Saturday," she offered.

"No, fair is fair. I *insist* on escorting you to your party, Friday night, as planned," Nick said firmly.

"All right then, if you insist," Emory replied. They agreed that Nick would pick her up at six o'clock on Friday night. As Emory hung up the phone, she had a sense of impending disaster that was by now a far too familiar feeling. You're being silly, she told herself. Everything is going to work out fine.

Emory kept repeating that phrase to herself, as if it were a mantra, throughout the long week. Finally Friday night arrived. Unfortunately the power of positive thinking did not prevail. She could see it from the very first moment that Nick arrived, almost an hour late, to pick her up. He had been working late on a case and hardly had time to comb his hair, no less change his clothes, or shave. He had remembered to put on a tie, at least. But it looked like one he stored under the front seat of his car, for emergencies such as tonight. Or maybe to wipe his windshield.

Academics dressed on the eccentric side, Emory reminded herself. Nick's disarray would hopefully blend right in. She was right about that part. His conversation, however, was quite another matter. While Emory had been quiet with his friends, having little in common with Emory's colleagues did not cause Nick to be the least bit subdued. If anything, he was going out of his way to strike up a conversation with anything standing in the room, including a potted palm.

"Your policeman friend is very…interesting," Cliff Lensky said to her at one point as they both spotted Nick across the room talking to Emory's department chairman. "He seems to have some very definite opinions," Cliff added in a subtly sardonic tone.

"Yes, he does," Emory said, defending Nick from this snob attack. "So do most people in this room," she pointed out.

"True," Cliff conceded. "How did you two meet? Speeding ticket?"

Emory was not allowed to say why she and Nick had really met. Not until the case was officially closed. Instead, she said, "Nick was in one of my classes. He's very interested in abstract impressionism," Emory added, thinking the interpretation was true enough.

"Really?" Cliff drawled skeptically. "I'll bet you two have some lively discussions," he said sarcastically. "I'll bet he keeps you up all night, Emory...talking about art, I mean."

Emory caught Cliff's snide inference and was infuriated. The nerve of this guy, insinuating that Nick was just some brainless, macho stud. Nick was braver, sweeter and even smarter in his way than Professor Cliff Lensky could ever hope to be, Emory fumed silently. What did she ever see in him?

"Nick and I have a lot to talk about," Emory sputtered angrily. "Daytime, nighttime, anytime."

"Oh...anyone can see that. No need to brag about your macho boyfriend," Cliff said cuttingly.

"Maybe I am," Emory said angrily. "There's a lot to brag about—" she blurted out, finally pushed over the edge by his insufferable snobbery.

"Emory—ready to go? I have an early day tomorrow," another voice cut into the heated conversation.

Nick stood beside her, looking very tired and grim. She could tell by one glance that he had overheard most—if not all—of her chat with Cliff. She only hoped he didn't misunderstand.

Emory said some hurried goodbyes as they left. They walked to the Jeep in silence and she sensed the storm clouds gathering between them.

"You were right. I shouldn't have come," Nick said finally as he began to drive her home.

"What are you talking about? Didn't you have a good time? You were talking to everyone," she observed.

"I was tracking them down and cornering them, you mean," Nick said with brutal honesty. "Nobody in that room really wanted to talk to me, unless they were curious about talking to a real cop."

"They were very interested to meet you. They all lead such sheltered, ivory-tower lives up there," Emory argued. "I was just a little surprised, I guess, at how outgoing you were. It's really a great trait," she added, forcing a smile. "You could go into politics."

In all honesty, she had felt uncomfortable with Nick's bold manner. The social gatherings of the art history department were so staid and regimented, Nick's straightforward manner had been as out of place as the appearance of a performing bear. They had reacted to him in approximately the same way they might have treated a performing bear, too, Emory speculated.

But that was just the way he had of dealing with a roomful of strangers. He charged straight in, made himself known. While she was more prone to try to blend into the woodwork.

"Why did you ask me to come with you if you didn't want me to talk to anybody?" Nick pressed her in a grim tone.

"Of course I wanted you to talk to people. I wanted you to talk to anybody you wanted to. I wanted you to have a good time. But if you didn't enjoy yourself with my colleagues, maybe you should just admit it," Emory countered.

They had arrived back at her street in record time. Nick pulled the Jeep up to a spot in front of her building, and came to a stop with his usual pit-stop landing.

"I embarrassed you, admit it. That's why you didn't want me to come with you tonight, too," Nick said, turning to her. She could see the hurt expression in his eyes and her heart felt like it was breaking into a million pieces.

"Nick, what are you saying? That's not true—" she argued.

"I heard your conversation with that history teacher," he said knowingly, "So don't try to deny it."

"I don't have anything to deny. Cliff Lensky is an insufferable snob and I suppose I lost my temper with him . . . and lost control of my tongue," she reflected. "But it has nothing to do with you . . . or with us."

"It has everything to do with us, Emory," he said, looking down at his hands gripping the steering wheel.

"Nick—please. Let's go inside. We need to talk. We can't settle this all out here in the car." She was pleading with him not to give up on their romance. But second by second, she felt the ground slipping away right under her, and she was powerless to do anything about it.

"I'd love to go inside with you," Nick said, breathing out a deep sigh. "But if we go up those steps, and through that door, we won't end up talking," he added on a wistful note. "You know it and I know it. Isn't that what you told your friend?"

"He's not my friend," Emory said angrily. "And that's not what I meant at all...." She hunched up on her side of the car, her arms crossed tightly over her chest. Why did he have to be so darned stubborn? Didn't he realize what he was doing? "You're making a mistake," she said finally. "We can work this out."

"I wish that was true," Nick said sadly. "I thought it was for a while. But I can see what's coming."

Emory turned to look at him. She knew it was useless to defend herself or try to explain her conversation with Cliff Lensky. Nick had been reminded too vividly of the problems in his last romance. How could she ever convince him that it could be different this time? Her behavior at the picnic had hardly been exemplary, she recalled with an inner cringe.

Maybe he just didn't want to be with her enough to try to work it out. Maybe her initial fears were coming true now, too. He was bored and looking for an easy way out. She was so confused, she didn't know what to think. Tears welled up in her eyes and blurred her vision. She got tangled in the seat belt as she tried to free herself.

"If that's the way you really feel," she said in a choked whisper, "I'm not going to sit here and...and beg you to talk it over—"

"Emory, please," he cut in, shaking his head. He sounded as if he was on the verge of tears himself. "I'm trying to do the right thing here. What's right for both of us in the long run. I've been through this before. It will hurt more later, believe me."

Emory couldn't imagine that it would hurt any more than it did right there and then. He was dumping her all right. Dumping her right on her own doorstep. Humiliating, but true. Gathering up her last shreds of pride, she blinked the tears away as she fumbled for the door handle.

"Maybe you're right. It was dumb of us to even try. A good story to add to your collection, I guess," she added bitterly.

"You have no right to say something like that to me. No right at all," he replied tightly. "You're better off with someone like Lensky, or your ex-husband, Wilfred—"

"His name is *Winston,*" she corrected him curtly. "And what makes you such an expert about the kind of man I should be with?"

"Plenty," Nick argued back. "I should have seen it from the start."

"Thanks for the advice. I'll keep it in mind," Emory said stiffly. She had finally revealed herself to someone—someone she believed she could trust—and this is what happened. He used all her most private frailties against her. His suggestions about suitable men sounded like a stinging insult and she couldn't help retaliating.

"Well, I think you'd be better off looking for dates at the gym next time. Or maybe at one of those sports bars with the big TVs all over the place—" Nick had taken her to a sports bar a few weeks ago to watch a baseball game and she'd ended up with a headache that lasted three days. At least she didn't have any more torturous outings like that to look forward to, thank goodness!

"Is that so?" Nick replied sharply. "Thanks for the tip. Maybe I should have gone there tonight to watch the Red Sox."

"Maybe you should have." Emory finally got the door open and jumped out. "Guess that's it, then. Bye,

Nick,'' she managed to say as she grabbed her purse off the floor.

"Emory—don't leave it like this—" He reached for her, his fingertips brushing her coat for **an** instant. But she quickly pulled away.

She ran up the steps and forced the front door open with one hard twist of the key. She turned and slammed the door hard behind her, catching a final glimpse of Nick as he stood at the bottom of the staircase, looking up at her. His hands were jammed into the pockets of his worn leather jacket, the streetlight illuminated his sad expression.

She wanted to turn, fly back down the stairs and into his arms. But she knew it wouldn't help solve the problems between them. Differences that had once seemed so funny, but now seemed so sad; their ultimate consequences, irrevocable.

Eleven

———

Emory spent the rest of the weekend alternating between weepy spells and fury at Nick's stubbornness, her own impulsive decision to get involved with him in the first place...and the forces of destiny in general.

By Monday morning, her mood swings had subsided enough for her to pack up things around her apartment that reminded her of Nick. It had only been a few weeks since they'd met, but her house seemed filled with reminders of him—little gifts he'd given her, a few articles of his clothes, CDs of jazz and blues artists he wanted her to listen to, a Boston Red Sox cap, a video cassette of his favorite episodes of twenty-year-old reruns. Too many reminders of the way he'd stepped into her life and changed everything, Emory thought sadly as she stowed the collected items in a big box.

She didn't regret having met Nick, or even taking a chance on loving him. He had taught her that great masterpieces weren't just hanging on museum walls—they were cooked in a kitchen, or in the way two people made love. And, she did love him. The saddest part was that she'd never even gotten the opportunity to tell him. She would never find another man that made her feel the way Nick did.

She had wanted to know true love and real passion for just once in her life. It just wasn't meant to last for very long, she tried to console herself. He didn't really have the feelings for her that he claimed. That was clear now.

Emory sniffed hard and blew her nose so loudly that Leo jumped up from a sound sleep on a pile of student term papers. The big orange cat strolled over to Emory and rubbed himself against her legs. She picked him up and stroked his head. "It's just you and me, pal," she told her faithful feline. "I'm sure you won't miss Nick chasing you off the bed."

The phone rang and Emory tossed the cat aside to dash over to her answering machine. She crossed her fingers and said a silent prayer that it was Nick. She wasn't going to pick it up, of course. Then he would know she'd been in all weekend, waiting for his call.

"Hello, Emory. This is Nolan Babcock," a deep smooth voice greeted her on the machine. "I've returned from Europe and I'm very eager to continue our discussion about the Newland collection. Why don't you call me at the gallery any day this week? I look forward to it. 'Bye for now…" There was a pause, then he said, "Oh, by the way, I hope you liked the flowers. Yellow tulips suit you, Emory. They really do."

When the message tone sounded and the machine rewound, Emory could feel the goose bumps popping out all over her skin. She'd almost forgotten all about Nolan Babcock.

Now she realized that she was the one who had to call first. But at least she had a valid excuse, she reminded herself. It was not like she was calling him up to reconsider his decision. The last meeting with Babcock was inevitable. It would be the last time she and Nick had to see each other. The sooner it was all concluded, the better, Emory thought.

She quickly dialed Nick's number at the station house and he answered on the first ring. "Fiore," he said, sounding even crankier than usual.

"Nick, it's me, Emory," she said, her words coming out in a rush. "I've just received a call from Nolan Babcock. You told me to call you immediately when he contacted me again," she said, reminding him that this wasn't a social call, she was just following orders.

"Yeah, sure," Nick answered with a distracted air. "Did you speak to him at all?"

"No, he left a message on my machine about ten minutes ago. He said I could reach him any day this week at his gallery."

"Did he mention the painting again?"

"Not really—"

"What does that mean?" Nick asked pointedly.

"He didn't mention it exactly," Emory said in a prickly tone. "But he did ask if I'd received his flowers."

"Oh, the flowers again." Nick sounded tired and irritated. "Too bad we can't collar this guy for sending flower arrangements." He sighed. "Listen, here's what you do. Can you come down to the station sometime today?''

"Uh, I can come at about two o'clock. What do I have to do there?''

"I want you to call him back from here, so that we can tape the conversation. You can thank him for the flowers, and then try to get him to mention the painting. Think you can do that?''

"I think so,'' Emory said hesitantly. She nervously twisted the cord around her fingers. "Will you be listening to the call?''

"I won't be, no,'' Nick said abruptly. "I've got another officer helping me with the case now. Marcy Dooley. Maybe you remember her from the picnic? Tall, red hair—''

"Oh, sure. She pitched the ball that I chased into the—''

"That's her,'' Nick cut in. He sounded rushed, as if he wanted to get her off the phone as fast as possible. "When you get here, just ask for Dooley. She'll know what to do,'' he said smoothly.

"Oh—all right. I'll do that,'' Emory said evenly, feeling teary again. He didn't even want to see her again, was that it? "Does that mean you're not on this case anymore?''

"I wouldn't say that I'm off the case exactly,'' he snapped. "But this isn't the only case I'm working on, for heaven's sake.''

"I only asked a simple question. You don't have to bite my head off.''

"I did not bite your head off. I simply answered your question,'' he replied with exaggerated restraint.

"Thanks for your time, Detective. It's been a pleasure chatting with you. As usual," Emory said as she angrily slammed down the phone.

Emory arrived at the station house precisely at two o'clock, lugging her carton of Nick's belongings. Marcy Dooley was waiting for her and greeted her as if they were old friends. Emory liked her and felt quite comfortable with her help for this part of the case.

Marcy led her to a room where a phone and tape recorder were already set up. She had an earphone headset at the same table, to listen in on the conversation and give her pointers if necessary.

Emory was nervous when she dialed Babcock, but the conversation went quite smoothly. They spoke briefly about the arts festival in Milan and his extended tour through Europe. As soon as she thanked him for the flowers, he again brought up the subject of the painting. Just as Nick had predicted he might.

"It's come to my attention that the work in question is available. To the right buyer, of course," he said finally.

"Could Mrs. Newland be the right buyer, do you think?" Emory asked him point-blank.

"It's possible—" he said slowly. "If she's prepared to make the financial commitment this type of special arrangement would require."

Marcy scratched "How much?" on a notepad and passed it to Emory. She nodded.

"How substantial a commitment would be required?" Emory asked.

"There have been previous offers, you know. Not nearly high enough, however. The work won't be moved from its present location for less than . . . eight million."

"That's too high," Emory said curtly. "We won't give you more than three for it."

She couldn't quite believe she was bargaining with a crook, but it was a part of her job that came automatically. She didn't even think twice before forming a counter offer.

Beside her, Marcy made a thumbs-up sign and approved her response with a big grin. "Good move!" she mouthed silently.

"Then perhaps this conversation is over before it's begun," Babcock said, sounding genuinely disappointed. "I thought Mrs. Newland had a serious interest in this work."

"But she does. She's very serious ... and willing to negotiate fair terms," Emory persisted, just hoping he wouldn't get cold feet and hang up.

"Fair terms, eh? All right, why don't we split the difference at five and a half, then? Is that fair-minded enough for you?"

She glanced at Marcy, who gave her an approving nod.

"I believe that figure will be acceptable to her," Emory said. Then, as she had been instructed, she pressed Babcock to make plans for the painting's delivery.

"We'd like you to deliver the package to my apartment, by Friday," Emory said, trying to sound as assertive as possible.

"Friday? To your home? That's not possible," Babcock said curtly.

"Why not?" Emory replied.

"It may take a few days to get the work out ... of storage. And I won't make the delivery to your home.

That's out of the question. I'll call you in a day or two with an alternative plan. How's that?''

Emory glanced at Marcy, who shook her head. "Get him to make a date," she scribbled on the pad.

"No, I need a firm answer right now," Emory pressed him. "The painting must be delivered by the weekend. Otherwise, the deal is off."

Babcock was silent for a long, tense moment. "Friday it will be, then," he said finally. "But not to your home."

"Where do you suggest?"

"I'll have a driver pick you up on Friday, at noon. He'll know where to take you. And only you," he emphasized. "You can leave that half-wit assistant of yours at home, if you don't mind."

Marcy slipped Emory another note. "Try to get him to say where."

"Where will I be meeting you? Mrs. Newland will want to know—"

"Don't worry, dear girl," Nolan cut in. "This is a simple business deal. How foolish do you think I am? You'll be returned to Mrs. Newland safe and sound, have no fear. She does want that painting, doesn't she?"

"Yes, of course," Emory replied.

"Well, then, just follow my instructions and she'll think you're a genius, won't she? By the way, this is how I want the money. Five hundred thousand in hundred-dollar bills in a single briefcase, please. A good leather bag would be a nice touch. Nothing tacky, I hope."

"Don't worry. We wouldn't dream of embarrassing you, Nolan," Emory replied cordially.

"I'm sure you won't," he replied smoothly. "The rest is to be deposited by twelve noon, eastern standard time, in a numbered account at the First Bank of Zurich. Have a pencil handy?" he asked casually.

With pencil poised, Marcy nodded at Emory.

"Go ahead—" Emory said, and Babcock gave her the number of his Swiss bank account. "Money can be moved around so easily these days with computers. I'm sure Mrs. Newland won't have any trouble arranging the transaction. See you Friday," Babcock added, then hung up the phone without waiting for Emory to reply.

Marcy pulled off her headset and gave out a loud whoop of laughter. "That was terrific, Emory. You were great."

Emory nodded and smiled, feeling shy from Marcy's lavish praise. "Your cues helped considerably. I never could have done it alone."

"Nonsense," Marcy said with a wave of her hand. "Wait till Nick hears this tape. He's going to love it."

"Oh, right. Nick," Emory said as she stood up and collected her belongings. "That reminds me, could you see that he gets this box?" she said, picking up the carton.

"Sure, I'll put it right on his desk," Marcy said agreeably. "Too bad we couldn't get Babcock to say where he was planning to close the deal, but he probably didn't figure out that part himself yet. Here's what you do once you get to the location—"

Marcy then explained the plan the police had worked out for Emory's meeting with Babcock. She had to insist on examining the painting before handing over the money. Once the painting and money changed hands, she would say "All's well that ends well" as a signal for the police to move in. Marcy made it sound very simple, like buying a pair of gloves at Bloomingdale's.

"The whole thing shouldn't take more than fifteen, twenty minutes, tops," she promised Emory. "We'll have a few cars following you. You won't see us, but we'll be there, believe me. Of course, we'll put a wire on you so we'll know what's happening every second. Did Nick tell you about that?"

"Yes, he did. When will you do that?"

"That's my job. I'll come by very early. Probably dressed as an exterminator or maybe wheeling a baby stroller. There's no telling if Babcock has someone watching your place."

"Yes, I guess that's possible," Emory said, feeling her skin crawl at the thought she was being spied upon.

"Starting today, we'll have someone outside, watching your house around the clock. Just in case."

"In case of what?"

"Just a precaution. We don't think Babcock is dangerous. But Nick didn't want you to worry. The police department does appreciate your help, Emory."

"Oh, well...the police department is very welcome, I guess," Emory said as she walked toward the door. It was some comfort to know that Nick was looking out for her welfare, even if he never wanted to see her again.

Emory spent the next few days feeling lonelier than she had ever felt in her entire life. Emory saw the car that Marcy had mentioned, a nondescript brown sedan, with a man sitting in the front seat reading a newspaper. It made her feel a little less on edge to know that some nameless policeman was out there. But for some reason, even lonelier.

She had never really minded living a secluded life before, but Nick had changed all that. She felt his absence with a deep and persistent pain. She waited each day for him to call her, even if it was only to talk over Friday's plans once more. But he never did.

She couldn't wait for Friday, for Babcock to arrive, get arrested and carted away. For this entire misadventure to be well and truly over.

On Friday morning at eight, her buzzer announced a visitor downstairs. Emory had been up since six, unable to sleep because she was so nervous. "Who is it?" she asked in a faltering voice.

"Exterminator, ma'am. Marcy Dooley," a familiar voice announced.

Emory hit the buzzer and let her in. Marcy stomped up the stairs with a spray can and canvas sack of tools. She was dressed perfectly for the part in a pair of gray overalls with a big roach embroidered on the pocket, and a baseball-style cap with the words Bug Bombers in big red letters on the brim.

"Let me at 'em," she greeted Emory.

A short time later, Marcy had fit Emory with a small microphone taped to her body under her clothing. The police receiver would be following in a van and could hear everything going on.

"Who will be in the van?" Emory asked.

"Me and two other guys, Benny Gonzalez and Rob Dodd."

Emory wondered where Nick would be. Was he even taking part in this phase of the case? But for some reason, she felt embarrassed asking Marcy about him.

"Hey, I almost forgot the money!" Marcy joked, reaching down into the sack. "Imagine that, I could

have had some shopping trip on my lunch hour today," she teased Emory.

She pulled out a large leather briefcase and opened
it up. Inside were stacks upon stacks of hundred-dollar
bills. "Looks good, doesn't it?" Marcy said with a
sigh. "There are some real ones on top, with phonies
mixed in on the bottom. Hopefully, he won't look that
closely. They rarely do," she added.

"It looks real enough to me," Emory said as Marcy
snapped the briefcase closed again. The police had also
arranged for a fake deposit in Babcock's bank account, Emory had learned on Thursday morning.

"You look a little pale," Marcy said sympatheti-
cally. "Didn't get much sleep last night, huh?"

"How did you guess?" Emory said, laughing.

"Don't worry, you'll do fine," Marcy assured her,
patting her shoulder. "Just stay calm and follow the
plan. We'll be right there when you need us."

"Right," Emory said, trying to sound calmer and in
control. Marcy left and Emory paced around the house
for the next few hours, waiting for her mystery ride. At
precisely noon, a long black limousine pulled up in
front of her house. A driver got out and rang her
doorbell.

"Mr. Babcock's car for you, Ms. Byrd," the man
said over the intercom.

"I'll be right down," Emory squeaked, her throat
getting suddenly dry and chalky.

Emory came downstairs, carrying the briefcase. She
glanced quickly up and down the street before getting
into the car. She had hoped to see the brown sedan, or
Marcy's exterminator truck. But the street looked ee-
rily empty.

The driver held the door open for her and she got in.
She felt as if she was about to disappear off the face of
the earth and no one would ever know what happened
to her. Her heart was pounding so loud she was sure it
was drowning out every other sound coming through
the microphone under her sweater.

She wanted to whisper a few words into the microphone, but was afraid the driver would hear her. Then
she had the bright idea of turning on the radio, which
she hoped would make it impossible to hear her up
front.

"Just testing," she whispered. "I hope you're out
there . . . somewhere," Emory added. She was tempted
to glance out the rear window, but knew that might
arouse the driver's suspicions.

The limousine glided through the city traffic, heading for the waterfront district. It reached the harbor
and drove along bumpy, cobblestone side roads between huge warehouses and closed-down shipyards. It
was a ramshackle and deserted part of the city that
Emory had never seen before.

Finally the car pulled up in front of a long wooden
pier. At the end of the pier there was a large wooden
warehouse. It looked as if it had been burned and
boarded up some time ago. It looked to Emory as if the
next strong storm could knock the whole structure into
the sea.

There was nothing else around for blocks and
blocks. Emory didn't even see another car. Where
could the police be? she wondered frantically. Had they
somehow lost her on the way?

The driver got out and opened her door. She grabbed
her briefcase and got out. A stiff cold wind blew her
coat open and she hugged it around her again.

"Where do I go?" she asked the driver.

"In there," he said, pointing to the broken-down building on the pier.

Emory turned and began walking. When she was a safe enough distance away, she whispered into the microphone again. "It's a pier, someplace outside the city. I can see two blue oil tanks not too far away and an island out in the water, directly ahead of this broken-down building. I don't see any cars... I wish I could see you..."

It was a long walk down the wooden pier, and difficult in heels, carrying the briefcase. Emory's hair, whipped by the wind, blew wildly across her face. She stopped in the middle of the pier and turned around to look back at the limousine. Her heart stopped beating when she saw that it was gone. How in the world did Babcock ever expect her to get out of here?

Twelve

Emory had no choice but to keep walking. "This will be some story to tell my grandchildren," she mumbled nervously into the microphone. "If I ever have *any* grandchildren."

She approached the warehouse and searched around for a likely opening or doorway. On the side of the building she found a door that wasn't boarded up. She pulled it open and stepped inside. It was so dark she could hardly see a few feet in front of her.

She took a step inside and then another. Her footsteps echoed in the unearthly silence. It was damp and cold, and the musty smell of rotting wood made her throat tighten. Emory could never recall being so scared in her life. She had a strong urge to simply turn and run out of the building, back out into the daylight and safety. But she forced herself to take yet another step into the darkness.

Something scurried past her feet, making a scratchy scuffling sound on the cement floor. "Ahh!" Emory shrieked and jumped back toward the door.

"Only a mouse," a deep voice, chuckling in the darkness, announced. "Or perhaps a rat."

"Nolan?" Emory called out. "Where are you? I can't see a thing."

"That's fine for now. I can see you. Show me the money."

At first the voice seemed to be coming from somewhere directly in front of her. Now it was coming from up above, she thought.

"It's right here." She held the case for him to see. "In this tasteful, designer case. All leather," she thought to add.

"Very nice." He finally stepped out of the shadows. He was standing very close to her and she hadn't even known it. "Put it on the table and open it up, so I can see what's inside," he insisted.

"What table?" Emory asked him.

"That one, right over there." His hand went to the wall. Across the room a small dim bulb that hung over a bare wood table flicked on.

"I need to see the painting first," Emory insisted, gripping the briefcase with two hands, as she had been instructed. "Where is it?"

"Right this way," Nolan said obligingly. He walked over to the table as if he was strolling down Park Avenue, Emory noticed. Did he carry on this sort of business everyday?

"Here it is." There was a long black plastic cylinder on the table, the type artists and draftsmen use to store and transport drawings. Nolan opened the cylinder and drew out what looked to be a rolled-up canvas. He carefully unrolled it on the table for Emory's inspection. "Beautiful, isn't it?"

"Just as I remember," Emory said as she drew closer to the painting. Her trained eyes scanned the canvas quickly but carefully. "One of the world's greatest treasures."

"And now it will be for Mrs. Newland's eyes only," Babcock reminded her. "You can open the case right on this chair," he added. More of an order than a suggestion, Emory realized.

As she walked a few steps to the chair, another unseen but sizable creature crawled around somewhere behind them. This one knocked something over, it sounded like an empty can.

"What the hell was that? I told you to come alone!" Before Emory knew what was happening, Babcock had his arm around her neck and a cold metal point stuck into her ribs.

"I am alone," Emory insisted, trying to pull away.

"Don't move a muscle," he said evenly.

"Wh-what's the m-matter with you, N-Nolan?" Emory stuttered. "It was just a rat, or something crawling around back there—"

"Well, well, what have we here?" Nolan said, his hand moving under her coat. Somehow his hand had felt the ridge of adhesive tape at her waist, beneath her sweater, she realized too late. Now his fingers searched knowingly for the thin wire from the microphone.

"Careful," she lied. "I have a broken rib."

"Looks like someone from the telephone company applied the first aid," he said blandly.

The gun barrel had moved from her ribs to her temple. Emory stared straight ahead. She thought she was going to pass out.

"Police. Drop the gun," a voice in the darkness behind them commanded.

Babcock whirled around to face his adversary, dragging Emory with him, the gun still pressed to her head. Nick stepped out of the shadows, holding his gun with two hands, pointed straight at Babcock. His face was as hard and grim as a stone mask.

"Let her go, Babcock. Or you don't have a prayer of leaving this building alive."

"I do with her as my escort," Babcock said. "She can even carry the money. Get the case," he ordered Emory, pushing her toward the briefcase.

Emory glanced over at Nick. Expressionless, he barely blinked at her. As Emory bent to reach the briefcase, a small space opened between the gun and her head. It was barely six inches and barely a split second of opportunity, but Nick reacted instantly, springing up from the shadows like a tiger.

Pushed aside, Emory fell hard, face first on the floor. His gun in his fist, Nick's arm swept up, striking Babcock hard under the jaw and knocking him back across the table. He grabbed Babcock's pistol arm and twisted it back over his head.

The police had told her about a thousand times that if there was trouble or guns, she was supposed to get down to the ground and try her best to get as far away as fast as possible. But Emory had to look up to see what was happening. The two men struggled, falling together across the table, as more police rushed into the building.

The gun went off and she screamed out loud when she realized Nick had been hit. He groaned, his body jerking back after the explosion. Blood appeared almost instantly, staining his shirtfront and running down his leg. But he wouldn't let go of Babcock, gripping the older man by the throat as he pressed him down against the table.

Seconds later, the other officers rushed to his aid. They grabbed Babcock by the arms and pulled him away. Emory rushed over to Nick, who was lying on the hard concrete. His eyes were squeezed closed with the pain and another officer was doing his best to stop the blood flow while they waited for an ambulance.

"Nick— My God—" Emory knelt down next to him and took his hand. A huge dark stain of blood covered his chest. He didn't open his eyes, but she could feel some pressure from his grip. "He's going to be all right, isn't he?" she asked the officer who was applying first aid.

"The gun was so damned close. Got right under the vest," the officer answered bluntly without looking up at her. "I think you'd better step back now, ma'am. The medical crew is here."

The emergency medical crew ran across the warehouse and surrounded Nick. Emory got up and stepped back out of their way. She was finally led out of the building by Marcy Dooley, who sat with her outside in a squad car.

Nick was quickly brought out on a stretcher, an IV tube with flowing blood attached to his arm. He was loaded into the back of an ambulance.

"Can you come with us down to the station, Emory? We'd like to get a statement from you," Marcy asked her.

"I need to go to the hospital. I have to see what happens to Nick," she insisted. The ambulance roared off the pier, its siren screeching and lights whirling.

Emory turned toward Marcy. "I want you to take me there. Please."

"We're really not supposed to—"

"Please," Emory said again.

Marcy stared at her and sighed. She reached into her purse and handed Emory a pack of tissues.

"Jack, follow Nick. They're taking him to Tufts-New England," Marcy told the officer driving the car.

The emergency room at Tufts-New England Medical Center was a chaotic scene. Nick was wheeled into surgery immediately. Reporters began to arrive a few minutes later, swarming the room with their mobile video cameras, trying to get some footage of the wounded police officer. Finally, a hospital spokesman briefed them on Nick's condition and persuaded them to go elsewhere for more information.

Emory was glad that no one had yet discovered her involvement. Marcy took her statement in the hospital coffee shop. Then Emory went back upstairs and hid behind a magazine near the surgery ward...and waited. Nick was in surgery for four hours. The bullet wound had been nearly fatal, shattering a rib and bypassing his heart by a scant half inch, a doctor finally explained to her. If he made it through the surgery, he had a good chance of making a full recovery, the doctor said.

She met his younger brother, Tom, who drove in from New York about eight o'clock that night. Tall and thin, with straight brown hair, Emory did not guess the relationship at first, until Tom smiled. Then she knew he had to be Nick's brother.

They stood together and watched Nick being wheeled from surgery into intensive care. Tom was obviously curious about her, Emory could tell. But it was hard to give anyone a clear idea of her relationship to Nick. She didn't really know what it was herself. Only that she loved him and could hardly stand waiting to find out if he'd be okay. But she would wait.

Finally, at about two in the morning, Emory was asleep in a chair when a nurse shook her shoulder. "He's waking up. You can go in to see him. But only for a minute," she warned.

Emory got up and followed the nurse. The waiting area was empty and dark. Nick's brother had gone downstairs in search of some coffee, the nurse told Emory. Emory was glad she would get to see Nick alone for at least a minute.

In the intensive care unit, Nick's bed was surrounded by cloth partitions. He was hooked up to about ten machines and had tubes running out of both arms, his nose, and even his mouth. Even though the nurse had said he was awake, his eyes were closed, his thick dark lashes resting on the dark shadows beneath his eyes.

Emory walked softly to his bedside. She rested her hand on his arm, the firm upper muscle that showed just below the half sleeve of his hospital gown. It was enough for her simply to feel him, alive and warm to her touch.

"Nick, I love you so much," she whispered. She leaned over and pressed her lips to his pale forehead. "Thank God you're alive."

She leaned back and looked at him. He didn't stir a muscle, his breathing slow and even. He was still asleep, after all, Emory realized. The anesthesia hadn't worn off yet. She stepped back from the bed, feeling dazed and relieved. Light-headed with relief that Nick was alive and going to be fine. The surgeon had told her that himself.

She'd finally told Nick that she loved him. She couldn't wait to say it again. When he was awake.

Thirteen

Visiting Nick was not a simple matter. He was in intensive care for several days and a tube down his throat prevented him from speaking to anyone. The only visitors he was allowed, Emory was told, were his brother or members of the police department. Although Emory tried her best powers of persuasion with the nurse in charge, she was simply not on the list.

About a week later, Emory found out that Nick was moved into a regular room, and most of the tubes and monitoring equipment had been removed. She tried calling him a few times, but each time she reached him, there was always some interruption, he claimed, providing a quick end to their conversation.

Determined to see him, she arrived at the hospital and asked for a visiting pass at the front desk. The attendant called up to Nick's room. Emory waited nervously, wondering if he would refuse to see her. That would be the final snub, wouldn't it? Would he actually do that to her?

Finally the desk attendant wrote her out a pass and told her how to find Nick's room. Emory knocked on the half-opened door, just to be polite. It was so quiet inside, she thought, perhaps the room was empty.

"Come in," Nick shouted from his bed.

She walked in slowly and smiled at him. "Hello, Nick. How are you?"

He was sitting up, wearing dark blue pajamas. His hair was combed back damply and neatly, an attempt to hide the fact that he badly needed a haircut, Emory thought. He had also grown a beard, which Emory found devastatingly attractive on him. He was still hooked up to an IV unit hanging near the bed, but otherwise he looked well on the road to recovery.

"I'm doing okay." He gave her a half smile. "That was a close one, but I squeaked by," he admitted. "Lucky break."

"Yes, you were very lucky," Emory said solemnly, thinking of how close she'd come to losing him. She was standing beside his bed and looked down at the blanket, unable to meet his gaze.

"Have a seat," he said hospitably. As he would to anyone, Emory thought as she sat down in a plastic chair near the bed. Not as if he'd been waiting to see her, or really cared for her anymore.

"So, you did your part for the Boston P.D.," Nick commended her. "We should have gotten in there sooner," he explained. "But Babcock had done some construction work, nailed up all the entries except for the one you came through."

"Really? How did you get in, then?" Emory asked.

"I—" Nick looked suddenly embarrassed, his cheeks flushing with color. "Well, when it sounded like you were in trouble, I came through the roof and crawled down some pipes," he explained. "It was easy in the dark," he added, making light of the effort.

"It doesn't sound very easy at all," Emory corrected him.

"Hey, that's my job, remember?" He nervously rubbed his beard and then smoothed out the blanket.

"What you did after that, leaping at Babcock and getting shot...that was very brave, Nick. You risked your life for me," Emory said. She tried to keep her voice under control, but couldn't entirely.

"It was nothing, really." He shook his head at her. Then looked down. "I was only doing my job. It wasn't especially brave. I just did what I knew I had to do."

"Oh, well, I wanted to thank you anyway," she said, seeing that he refused to bring any element of personal feeling into the conversation.

"You're very welcome," he said with a nod, looking down at his blankets again. "That's what cops are for, right?"

"I suppose—" Emory shifted in her chair. Her heart sunk like a lead weight.

This was hardly the meeting she had envisioned. For the past few days, Emory imagined that she would throw her arms around his neck and show him how worried she'd been that he would die. That she realized how foolish and trivial their argument had been, when she thought she'd never see him again. He would tell her that he'd reached the same conclusion. And he had done whatever it took to save her that day, even risking his own life, because he loved her.

Emory wanted to say all those things, and more. But she didn't know how to begin. "Nick, I want to talk to you about something," she said in a faltering voice. "Something important—"

"I got that box of stuff you left with Marcy Dooley, by the way," he said then, cutting her off. The hard look he gave her then robbed Emory of any shreds of courage she had gathered to tackle his resistance.

"I guess I was angry with you," she admitted. "I wish now I had kept all those things a little longer. I wish I had called you to come and pick them up," she added.

Nick looked at her quizzically, his expression showing the first hopeful sign, she thought. There was a brisk knock on the door and the doctor entered the room. "Mr. Fiore, time to take a look at your incision, I'm afraid."

"What are you afraid of? You're a doctor, aren't you?" Nick replied with a characteristic wisecrack.

"You're in fine spirits today, Nick," the doctor said, showing little reaction to Nick's irreverence.

"You'll have to leave while the patient is being examined," a nurse told Emory.

"Sorry to chase your visitor away," the doctor told Nick. He glanced up at Emory as he checked Nick's chart. Nick sat up and began to unbutton his pajama top. Emory nearly gasped, seeing the length of the long incision beneath the bandage. The stitching stretched from his upper right shoulder, down past the waistband of his pajama bottoms.

"She was just leaving," Nick said curtly. "Weren't you?"

"Uh, yes." Emory stood up quickly. "Goodbye Nick. Get better soon," Emory murmured as she headed for the door.

"So long...Professor," she heard Nick call after her.

After visiting Nick, Emory felt completely discouraged. There seemed to be no possibility at all, she thought, that they would ever manage to get back together. Nick didn't want to have anything to do with her. He obviously wished she would just disappear. She called the hospital every day to see how he was progressing, but never asked to speak with him again. A nurse had told her that he was due to be released in a day or two. Emory felt relieved to hear that, then saddened that she wouldn't be the one taking care of him as he recovered. Who would it be? Some hired nurse's aid? His brother? Some old girlfriend he'd call to cheer him up?

Emory knew she was torturing herself with speculation, but couldn't seem to help it. She was working late in her office one night, mulling over such thoughts, when the phone rang.

"Professor Byrd? This is Tom Fiore," a deep voice, exactly like Nick's said. "We met at the hospital the night they brought Nick in?" he reminded her.

"Of course. I remember you," Emory said. Then quickly added, "Nick is okay, isn't he? Nothing's gone wrong?"

"Oh, he's fine. A little too restless for his own good, in fact. The hospital can't handle him anymore. They're sending him home tomorrow."

"That's great," Emory said sincerely. "I'm very happy to hear that."

"The reason I'm calling," Tom continued smoothly, "is that I wondered if you could do me a small favor, being a special friend of Nick's and all...."

Who had told him that she was Nick's "special" friend? Certainly not Nick.

"What sort of favor?" Emory asked curiously.

"Well, I'm picking Nick up at about ten tomorrow morning and bringing him back to his place. But I have to get back to New York by the afternoon. I'm about to begin a trial and really can't spare much more time in Boston," he explained.

"Oh, I see," Emory said, even though she really didn't see what he was getting at.

"I wanted to give you the key to Nick's place, so you could go there and straighten things up a bit. Put some groceries in the fridge. That sort of thing?"

"Sure, I can do that." Emory had no problems with that. But why her? Nick seemed to have about a thousand other friends who'd be a more likely choice.

"And would you mind staying there awhile in the afternoon, when I bring him back? To keep him company?" Tom added.

"Tom—" Emory hesitated. "Why are you asking me to do this? Nick has plenty of friends he'd rather see much more than me."

"No, I think you're wrong. He's talked to me about you," Tom admitted. "He'd kill me if he knew I was telling you...but what are brothers for?" he asked playfully.

"If he's talked to you, I'm sure he's told you that we decided not to see each other anymore."

"Sure, he told me that part. But from the rest of it, and the things he said, especially after you came here last week to see him—" Tom sighed. "He needs you to be there for him tomorrow. Trust me. He's just too damned stubborn to admit it.''

''I think he'll be angry,'' Emory said. She wanted nothing more than to be the one-woman welcoming-home committee for Nick tomorrow. But she was afraid of his reaction and how much it would hurt if he asked her to go. She didn't think she could stand being hurt much more by him.

''Trust me. Please?'' Tom said again. His voice sounding so much like Nick's, it was hard for Emory to resist giving in instantly. ''You owe it to him to try, one more time. You owe it to yourself,'' Tom added.

Emory sighed, knowing in her heart he was right. ''When can I pick up the key from you?''

The next morning, Emory paced Nick's apartment nervously. It was already eleven-thirty and no sign of Nick and his brother. The house was spotlessly clean, with fresh sheets, towels and a big bowl of flowers in the middle of the living room. The kitchen was stocked with all the foods Nick liked to eat.

Emory had also bought all the ingredients for one of his favorite dishes, calamari. The plastic container of wriggly looking tentacled squid was sitting on the top shelf of the refrigerator while she studied some cookbooks she'd gotten out of the library.

She checked the way she looked in the mirror about ten times in five minutes. She was wearing black stirrup pants and a dark red pullover, an outfit that Nick had once told her he liked very much. Pushing it aside, Emory wore her hair loose. She put on a pair of big brass earrings Nick had dared her to buy when they were down in Soho during their trip to New York.

Finally she heard Nick and Tom coming into the apartment's front entrance. She wondered if Tom had mentioned she'd be there, but when Nick stepped through the door, she could see from his shocked expression that Tom hadn't said a thing.

"Hi, Nick. Welcome home," Emory said.

"For Christmas' sake—" He blinked and shook his head, as if his vision was playing tricks on him. "Tom, you son of a . . ." He turned, looking for his brother. "You want to give a guy a heart attack?" he railed at him.

"Oh, shut up for a minute, will you?" Tom called back at him as he prodded Nick inside and closed the door. "Dad always said you had a big mouth, Nick," he added.

"Look who's talking." Nick laughed. "You're the legal mouthpiece, if I need to remind you."

"Which reminds me—" Tom glanced down at his watch "—I'm due in court in less than three hours. If you're all settled in here, Nick, I guess I'll be on my way," Tom said smoothly, moving toward the door. "Emory, nice job. Those flowers are very pretty."

"Hey, not so fast!" Nick yelled out to his brother.

"Take it easy now, Nick. You're still recovering," Tom reminded his older brother with a quick pat on Nick's good shoulder. "I'll speak to you later," he said, and disappeared out the door like a rabbit hopping down a rabbit hole.

They were suddenly and completely alone. Nick collapsed in a big leather couch. Emory realized that he was hardly at his full strength and probably still on painkillers.

"Do you need anything?" she asked him quietly.

"Yeah, a new set of relatives. Ones that don't butt in with my life so much," he grumbled.

Emory walked closer and stood by the couch. "I'll go if you want. I'll call someone to come over and stay here with you instead," she offered quietly.

"No—wait a minute—" He reached up and took her hand. "I don't want you to go. It's just that I was so surprised to see you when I walked in. I thought I was having a hallucination or something, from the drugs I've been taking," Nick said with a laugh.

"A good hallucination...or a bad one?" Emory asked. Coming around to face him, she sat down next to him.

"A good one...a great one," he said quietly. "A dream come true. Like the dream I had after the surgery, from the anesthesia," he added, more to himself than to her.

"Oh—" She was so startled she didn't know what to say. "I love you," she said suddenly. It just came out. "I've had a lot of time to think. I can't even remember what we argued about or why we split up. Nothing important. Not as important as how much I love you."

Nick stretched out his arms and pulled her close. She had to be careful not to hug him too hard because of his injury, but she pressed her face to his chest, fitting her head neatly under his chin.

"I love you, too," he said. "I nearly went crazy when Babcock pulled that gun on you. I thought I was going to break right through the roof. I could have killed that guy when he touched you," Nick said, getting all worked up over the memories.

"Shh," Emory soothed him. "It's all over now. We're both okay."

"Luckily," Nick sighed. "When you came to see me in the hospital, I knew you were grateful. But I didn't think you could forgive me for all the things I said to you after that party. I was just so sure you'd eventually dump me, I had to dump you first. I'm a jerk," he observed of himself.

"Hmm, sometimes," Emory agreed playfully. "So am I."

"No you're not," Nick said, kissing the top of her head.

"Well, I pouted at the softball game. I was like a spoiled little girl," she pointed out.

"Well—since you brought it up," he said. "I guess that's true."

"It is true. And we are very different. But I've given this a lot of thought the last few days. We don't have to like everything the other person likes. That's just superficial."

"Yes—it is," Nick agreed. "We share something much deeper, sweetheart," Nick said. "I know that now. The other stuff—well, it will get on our nerves from time to time, I'm sure. But it really doesn't matter. Not to me, at least."

"Not to me, either," Emory agreed, holding him close. For the first time, Emory finally felt free of her worries about Nick. She might never be able to say exactly why she and Nick were so right for each other. It was a connection that went far deeper than their taste in clothes, music or pastimes. But as unlikely as it seemed, they were a perfect match. She not only loved him, she respected and admired him. She would always be proud that he loved her and knew now that he felt the same.

"We'll have a big party when you're feeling better. All your friends . . . and mine," she proposed.

"That will be some party," Nick said. "But I refuse to invite my brother Tom. He was always playing pranks on me when we were kids, but this one is over the top."

"Oh, well. If you don't want to, he's your brother," Emory said, she knew that once Nick had some time to think about it, he'd not only forgive his brother, he'd probably send him flowers.

"On second thought, I guess we will have to invite him," Nick said, rubbing Emory's back in a sensuous caress. "Can't have a wedding without a best man."

Her head popped up and she looked at him, their faces inches apart. "Is this a proposal of marriage?"

"You bet. The real thing. For life. Professor Emory Byrd-Fiore," he announced slowly, testing the sound. "What do you think?"

"I love it," she said, kissing him hard on the mouth. "It looks good written out, too," she added, admitting that she had tried the name on for size before his proposal.

"You know, in the police department, we have *excellent* benefits," he teased her.

"Yes, I know," Emory murmured, nuzzling his ear. "I'm already acquainted with a few."

Nick made more room for Emory to stretch out on the couch beside him. Too bad he was still not fully recovered, she thought. She could make love to him for days. However, they managed to kiss and caress each other as much as his injury would allow. It was only a tantalizing preview of the lovemaking to come, once Nick was recovered, and both of them had to laugh at their frustration.

"I love you so much," Nick whispered tenderly as he held her close. "I'm never going to let you leave me again."

"I never will," Emory promised, sealing their bargain with a deep kiss.

Later, while Nick sat on a comfortable chair, supervising, Emory began methodically chopping up onions and garlic in preparation for their dinner. It was her first attempt at cooking anything more complicated than scrambled eggs and she hoped it didn't show too much. She had so many cookbooks spread out around her on the countertops and table, that Nick said there wasn't any room left for the food.

"I was down at the station house yesterday," Emory said. "Examining the painting."

"Really? Nobody told me about that," Nick said. "I guess the museum will be thrilled to have it back."

"They would be," Emory said. "But I had to tell them that the painting Babcock tried to sell me was a fake."

"It was? How do you know?"

"Believe me, I know. A clumsy job at that," Emory assured him. "I was almost sure the first time I saw it in the warehouse, but it was so dark and everything was happening so fast."

"Well, I'll be damned." Nick shook his head. "That old weasel. He'll still do time, though, fake or not."

"But that means the real one is still out there someplace," Emory reminded him.

"Wait a second—" Nick caught the gleam in her eye and guessed what she was thinking. "Your detective days are over, Professor. This was your first and last case, if I have anything to say about it."

"Nick, come on. We nearly had it," she reminded him.

"Forget it. I hope that painting is in Singa-pore...or Tierra del Fuego...or anywhere clear out of my territory."

"Maybe it is," she said agreeably. She turned back to her cooking, one of Nick's favorite jazz musicians, Miles Davis, was on the stereo. She had a feeling that after a good meal and some wine she might be able to change Detective Fiore's mind about this matter. She would give it her best effort—her best, most loving, and sensual appeal to his sometimes stubborn side. Nick was a challenge, but Emory knew now that meeting that challenge was the real art of love.

*   *   *   *   *

NORA ROBERTS

Love has a language all its own, and for centuries, flowers have symbolized love's finest expression. Discover the language of flowers—and love—in this romantic collection of 48 favorite books by bestselling author Nora Roberts.

Starting in February, two titles will be available each month at your favorite retail outlet.

In February, look for:

Irish Thoroughbred, **Volume #1**
The Law Is A Lady, **Volume #2**

In March, look for:

Irish Rose, **Volume #3**
Storm Warning, **Volume #4**

Collect all 48 titles and become fluent in

THE LANGUAGE of LOVE

LOL292

Take 4 bestselling love stories FREE

Plus get a FREE surprise gift!

The Case of the
Mesmerizing Boss
DIANA PALMER

Diana Palmer's exciting new series,
MOST WANTED, begins in March with
THE CASE OF THE MESMERIZING BOSS....

Dane Lassiter—one-time Texas Ranger
extraordinaire—now heads his own group of
crack private detectives. Soul-scarred by
women, this heart-stopping private eyeful
exists only for his work—until the night his
secretary, Tess Meriwether, becomes the target
of drug dealers. Dane wants to keep her safe.
But their stormy past makes him the one man
Tess *doesn't* want protecting her....

Don't miss THE CASE OF THE MESMERIZING
BOSS by Diana Palmer, first in a lineup of
heroes MOST WANTED! In June, watch for THE
CASE OF THE CONFIRMED BACHELOR...only
from Silhouette Desire!

MOST WANTED